ADVANCE PRAISE FOR

THE ANIMAL GAZER

“This poignant and emotiona [illegible]
sive and elegant prose, and [illegible] to readers of
historical and literary fiction, as well as those interested in
early twentieth century artists.”

—*IndiePicks Magazine*

“A moody, impressionistic, and strangely engaging work.”

—*Kirkus Reviews* (Starred Review)

“*The Animal Gazer* takes you on a glorious journey into the heart of cosmopolitan Paris as you have never known it before. Through the life of Rembrandt Bugatti, a sculptor with the panache of his name, this lively, fast-paced narrative evokes an exceptional epoch in all its color and eccentric charm.”

—NICHOLAS FOX WEBER, author of *Balthus: A Biography*; *Le Corbusier: A Life* and *Patron Saints: Five Rebels Who Opened America to a New Art*

“An unusual story about a gifted but doomed young artist that grows in poignancy as it accelerates towards its tragic end.”

—MICHAEL PEPPIATT, author of *Francis Bacon in Your Blood* and *In Giacometti’s Studio*

"This wonderful book not only tells the life of a great sculptor, it is also a testimony to the devastation that every war brings to the life of men and artists."

—IL FATTO QUOTIDIANO

"Edgardo Franzosini is among the finest contemporary Italian writers ... Franzosini illuminates the life of this singular artist ... an artist capable of sculpting in bronze the movements of animals and grasping their vitality in such a way that critics, after years of neglect, are discovering its unique power."

—IL GIORNALE

"So well documented and psychologically penetrating that the entire book gives the reader the feeling of an autobiographical testimony."

—LIBERO

"A book that hurts but with a beauty and humane poetry that allows for nostalgia and sweetness."

—LA VOCE DI PISTOIA

THE ANIMAL GAZER

EDGARDO FRANZOSINI

TRANSLATED BY
MICHAEL F. MOORE

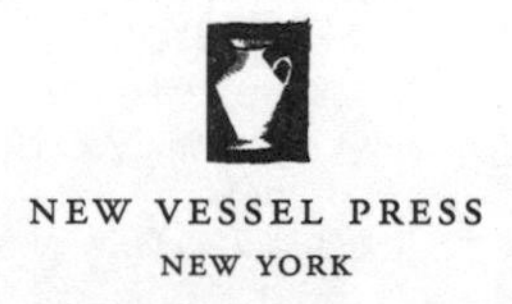

NEW VESSEL PRESS
NEW YORK

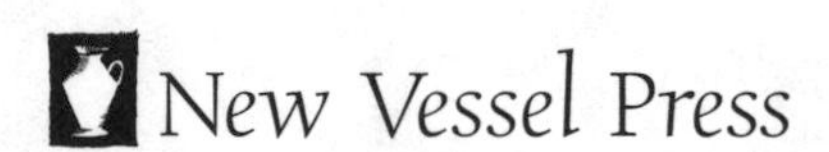

First published in Italy in 2015 by Adelphi Edizioni, Milan, as
Questa vita tuttavia mi pesa molto

This edition published in agreement with Piergiorgio Nicolazzini Literary Agency (PNLA)

Library of Congress Cataloging-in-Publication Data
Franzosini, Edgardo
[Questa vita tuttavia mi pesa molto. English]
The Animal Gazer/ Edgardo Franzosini; translation by Michael F. Moore.
p. cm.
ISBN 978-1-939931-52-8
Library of Congress Control Number 2017907474

I. Italy — Fiction

THE ANIMAL GAZER

I

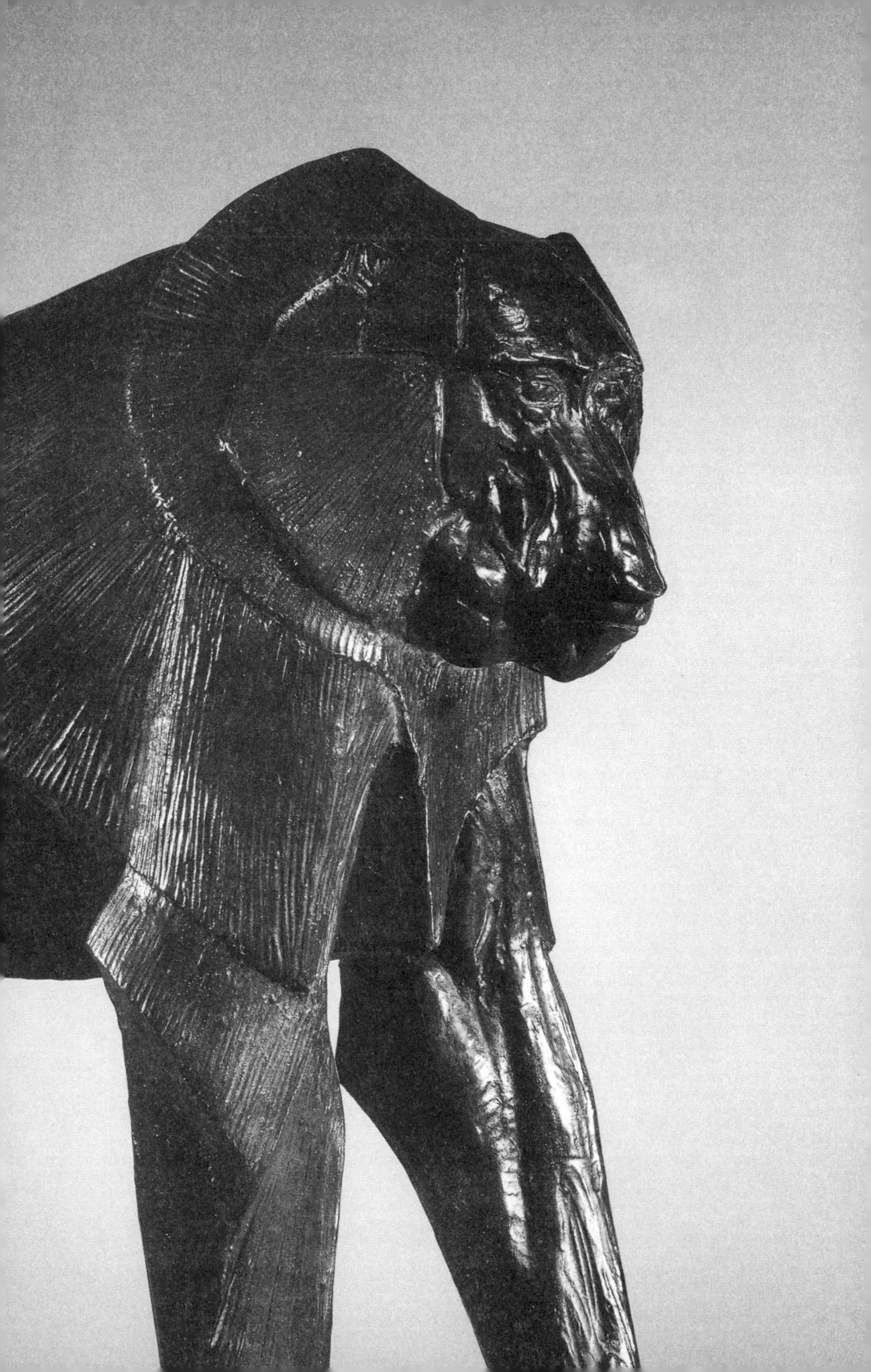

By the main door of 3 Rue Joseph-Bara, a lead-gray building with a tile roof that had lost all its former elegance, Madame Soulimant, the concierge, was sitting, as usual. There, by the main door, she would spend most of the day—and in summer often some of the night as well—shifting her cane-bottomed chair from the right to the left of the small arched entrance, depending on the hour.

"Good morning, Monsieur Bugatti," she said, turning to a man passing through the entrance.

The man replied courteously, doffing his wide-brimmed black felt hat, revealing a broad and prominent forehead. He was tall and elegantly dressed, but his shoulders were stooped and his gait stiff and awkward. (According to his friend André Salmon, when he walked he gave the impression of wanting to shun people if not avoid them altogether.)

"Can you believe this weather, good heavens! Not a very promising start for the fall!" said the concierge, huddling in a sheepskin shawl, dirty and yellow, that Madame Soulimant would drape over her shoulders at the first sign of cold weather. "I read in *Le Matin* that it's the cannon shots, the artillery fire. That's what's causing the rain!"

"Really?" asked Rembrandt Bugatti.

"Yes, the cannons cause the rain as surely as the moon sways the weather!" replied Madame Soulimant, with a slight turn of her head, her frizzy gray hair tied behind her neck in a loose bun.

Rembrandt also read the news of the war every day in the pages of *Le Matin* and *Le Petit Journal*. The week before one item in particular had caught his attention. The Siegesallee was a broad boulevard in Berlin lined with thirty-two monumental marble statues depicting the Margraves, the Prince Electors, the Dukes and Kings of Brandenburg and Prussia, and the ancestors and predecessors of Wilhelm II. At one end a wood and plaster totem had been raised bearing the same features as General Hindenburg. *L'Illustration* reported, "At night it is illuminated by three hundred torches and its shadow is projected down the entire length of the avenue. And to assure that the spirit of war and victory, 'the sovereign with echoing arms,' is on their side, the people of Berlin have been invited to stick at least one nail in the figure. It costs one hundred marks to insert one golden nail, thirty for a silver nail, and only one mark for steel."

"And meanwhile," added Madame Soulimant, "the Germans continue to advance. Soon they'll be here."

"HAVE YOU BEEN to the market, Monsieur Bugatti?" the concierge asked the tenant, speaking a little louder so as to be heard.

Chronic otitis had made Rembrandt almost deaf. One year earlier he had started to feel painful spasms, whistling, humming and his own voice echoing in his ears. Sounds had all started to blur into a single drone. The only thing he could still distinguish were the sounds of animals—trumpeting, roaring, whinnying—at the thought of which he could not hold back a smile. A white liquid had started to ooze down his cheeks on occasion. An ailment of this type was still considered insignificant, almost healthy, as his doctor told him, but there could be many serious complications: meningitis, perforation of the carotid artery, cerebral hemorrhage. This is why, after administering him a compound of sulfate and sodium salts, the doctor prescribed hot compresses on the ear, fumigations, and gargling.

"Yes, first to Mass and then to market. You can't find a thing there, you know. Four eggs and a crust of bread," Bugatti replied. If not for a few overly guttural *r*'s, Bugatti's French would have been perfect: by then the accents fell naturally on the right places. Besides, more than twelve years had gone by since he had left Milan and Italy and decided to split his time between France and Belgium, going back and forth: a few years in Paris, a few years in Antwerp.

"Don't mention bread," said Madame Soulimant, "the thought of it makes my tongue swell and gives me pains in the chest and kidneys . . . worst of all, forgive me for saying this, after eating bread I can't stop burping."

Rembrandt shrugged his shoulders.

On their way out to Rue Joseph-Bara, all kinds of people had passed through the entrance, which reeked of cabbage soup, turpentine, rancid ham, and urine.

And so many artists! as Madame Soulimant remarked with a certain pride. She had this to say about Paul Gaugin: I remember him, a big tall man. He was no brute, but he was always excited, talking in a loud voice, and he never closed the main door behind him. As for Jules Pascin: the only time he ever opened his mouth was to ask if the mail had arrived. Most of the time he was so drunk he could barely stand up. Is there a letter for me? he would ask on his way in or out. How annoying! Any postcards today, Madame Soulimant? A telegram, perhaps? In many long years no one ever sent him anything. An impudent conceited little Bulgarian. Nothing like you, Monsieur Bugatti.

Madame Soulimant liked this distinguished, reserved man with his angular face and serious expression. (Years later, seeing an actor at the cinema whom the French used to call Frigo but later became world famous as Buster Keaton, Madame Soulimant could not help but reminisce on the sad face of that tenant.)

"Well, have a good day," said Bugatti.

"And a good day to you," replied the concierge, placing her hands over her breast and lowering her gaze to the pointed black patent leather shoes with a brass monk strap that, despite the rain, Bugatti wore every day. He had on an overcoat that reached almost all the way to the ground. He opened it slightly to reach inside and dig out the apartment keys from a pocket in his black and white checked jacket, revealing a pair of rather wide gray corduroy trousers, almost puffy around the hips, which suddenly narrowed at the knee to end in a tube shape around the ankles.

What elegance, what refinement, thought the concierge. Only princes, marquises, or dukes dress this way, she thought. And it was no slip of the tongue, when she happened to speak to someone else about him, that she called him the Aristocrat. Monsieur Bugatti, the Aristocrat, is also an artist, a sculptor, she would tell people, but he never invites models up to his studio. That way she didn't have to worry about anyone leaving muddy shoeprints on her stairs.

Rembrandt Bugatti's friends—the ones whom he occasionally, but now more and more rarely, frequented at the Closerie des Lilas—called him the American. Not because he had the strong, active, energetic air of a man who practices the more vigorous sports, but maybe simply because of his height, together with the serene insolence of his gaze. Or maybe because as soon as he had his hands on some money, Rembrandt would spend it, the same way they imagined all Americans do.

In one jacket pocket he still had his last invoice from Guillemet et Fils: one pair of gloves, 150 francs; one hat, 450 francs; two shirts, 600 francs; one necktie, 120 francs;

three pairs of socks, 180 francs. He rested his eyes on the piece of paper and thought: I'll have to ask Ettore to lend me some money. His brother had always helped him. And Rembrandt, for his part, had always paid him back. He loved Ettore as well as his wife and children: Ebé, Lidia, and Jean. Ettore was his older brother. Some years back Rembrandt had helped him to bury three car engines in the yard behind the sumptuous villa that he owned in Molsheim, in German Alsace, right across the border, next to the big workshop where Ettore built his automobiles.

THANKS TO A safe-conduct granted at the insistence of Count von Zeppelin, a friend of Ettore and the inventor of the dirigible then being used to dispense death from the sky, Rembrandt and Ettore reached Strasbourg by train, passing through Switzerland. A taxi left them in front of the workshop gate.

"First let's go in the house for a moment," suggested Ettore, "but without turning the light on. Too dangerous."

In the dark, Ettore went from room to room, while Rembrandt, patient and silent, followed close behind. His brother seemed to be inspecting them for traces of a stranger who had passed through, and he appeared surprised, almost amazed, that everything had remained exactly as he had left it at the time of his hasty departure.

"Well, only a few months have gone by," admitted Ettore, in a resigned and melancholic voice, as if an entire century had elapsed. "I left everything here."

Rembrandt looked at a corner of the parlor where in the dim light he could make out the outline of a guitar, seven feet high, with at least thirty strings. Rembrandt approached it and with one finger plucked a string: *blen!* That outsized instrument had been created by his father's hands. (It was not the only outsized and unconventional thing that his father, Carlo, had built: armoires upholstered in camel skin; throne chairs with asymmetrical spindles, vellum inlays, and copper and bone appliqués; one-wheeled buggies; mirrors framed in donkey hide; stools shaped like boa constrictors.)

"Help me carry this to the workshop," said Ettore, indicating the guitar, "it'll be safer there. Unless we want to bury it, too, in some part of the garden," he added, but without smiling. Ettore lowered the guitar slowly until it was lying flat on the floor. "You take the neck, I'll take the body," he told Rembrandt.

The two left the house. It was a moonless autumn night. The workshop, only slightly less dark than the night, was a few steps away. Inside the stench of grease melted into the smell of gas and the sickly sweet odor of rubber tires. Only one automobile was left: the Tipo 10.

"The tub," said Ettore. Which is what the two brothers called it.

"The old tub," repeated Rembrandt. And he thought back to the day when he was photographed behind the wheel of the Tipo 10 with his back straight, rigid, his long legs folded and a melancholic smile.

"Let's put it here, inside the tub," said Ettore.

The guitar was wedged between the seat and the windshield. The body bumped against the backrest, and a dark, deep, amplified sound was released into the still air of the workshop.

"Now for the engines," said Ettore.

Along a wall, one next to the other, three engines were lined up.

"We need some blankets," added Ettore, and he went off to look for some in the house.

In the meantime Rembrandt sat down on a stack of tires in a corner of the workshop. Through the big window he could see the house. This time his brother had turned on the lights. It would appear that the search for blankets was not so easy.

When he returned Ettore said, "I found two blankets and a tablecloth. They'll have to do."

The tablecloth was made from burgundy velvet, with a fringed border. They wrapped the engines carefully and then took them outside and laid them on the grass, under a beech tree. Ettore circled the yard for a while, looking for the best place to dig.

"Here, next to the boxwood hedge," he said to Rembrandt, "the ground doesn't seem as hard."

With the shovels they dug three five-foot deep holes. Then, with a delicacy suitable for an inhumation, they lowered the three automobile engines into the holes, one after the other, and covered them back up with soil.

...

No model, male or female, had ever gone upstairs to Rembrandt Bugatti's studio.

What a face Madame Soulimant would have made if she had seen the models for Bugatti's sculptures enter through the front door of Rue Joseph-Bara and climb the stairs that she scrubbed once every two weeks with a mixture of wood ash and boiling water: pelicans, antelopes, leopards, Nubian lions, Indian rhinoceroses, Grant's gazelles, elephants, pythons, tigers, jaguars, deer, condors, bison, anteaters. Rather it was Rembrandt who travelled to his models, which lived behind the bars of the zoo. And he gazed with envy at the animals' blissful ignorance. Every day he would take the street leading from Rue Joseph-Bara to the Jardin des Plantes, the Paris zoo, crossing Boulevard Saint-Michel and Rue Saint-Jacques. Rembrandt felt like himself only around animals, only in contact with that wordless community. The zoo is my consolation, he wrote one day to his brother. When I am in front of them and they stare me in the eye, he told his mother, I feel—please don't laugh—as if I understand perfectly their joys and their sorrows. I know it might sound silly, sentimental, he said, baffled by his own words, but that's how it is.

When the Jardin des Plantes opened to the public, at around ten o'clock in the morning, and the animal moved from the back of its cage (sometimes it was forced to the front by pushes and shoves) before the stares of the crowd, on the makeshift stage where it performed every day, Rembrandt, too, stopped by the cage and sat on a bench. If there was a bench. Otherwise he remained standing, but without taking his eyes off the animal. As if he wanted to understand the nature of its thoughts, or rather, as if he wanted to get under its skin.

On some of the animals the fur was shiny and the nostrils wet. Animals that had been robbed of the joy of blood, the lust for tearing their prey limb from limb. Animal life, thought Rembrandt with an obscure sadness, perhaps, and fortunately, does not demand a huge amount of learning, does not demand long and complex efforts.

Bugatti was able to observe some of his models from a privileged vantage point: the spot where the animals withdrew at night to sleep, or by day to rest, napping while waiting for the wardens to bring them their food. The cages were hidden from the eyes of the public. In those dimly lit and poorly cleaned corridors, echoing with animal sounds, Rembrandt was allowed to enter and remain all day. The animals seemed to pay him no mind, nor did the zookeepers, with whom Rembrandt would mingle starting early in the morning, from the moment the animals got their first meal. They would cast a glance at him and think they had seen stranger things.

Rembrandt would set himself up there, sitting on an empty bucket turned upside down that had originally held the animal feed. His long legs bent, his hands resting on his knees. At that hour of the morning his mind was clear and his senses sang to the breaking point. The smell of the animals mixed in with the equally acrid stench of the food, not to mention the fetid odor that emanated from the fur balls regurgitated by the felines. Swarms of flies flew in the air, flitting around his forehead, his mouth, his hands. But this didn't seem to deter Rembrandt, who would spend all morning observing the animals' movements or contemplating them when they retreated, sated, to a corner of the cage. Sometimes his face was almost distorted by a frown, so intense were his efforts at concentration. He would remain motionless to decipher the bodies of animals with the eyes of a sleepwalker, his face dripping in sweat, as if he were about to cross an invisible border. The most important thing was not to frighten them. Learn to approach them without frightening them. It didn't take much for them to be seized by panic. And then they might react by fleeing, attacking, or standing perfectly still—and for Bugatti this last possibility was no less unpleasant than the others. They need to get used to my presence, he thought. And I need to know exactly what the minimum distance is for each to keep them from reacting in one of these three ways.

At the Jardin des Plantes, Rembrandt befriended one of the keepers, Monsieur Moussinac. No one knows the animals better, he thought, than the people who live in daily contact with them. Moussinac was assigned to the carnivores, and at a certain time of day he would stop by the zoo's butcher and fill up his pushcart with chunks of meat. Donkey meat most of the time. Then he would push the cart to the area where all the big cats were located. Their cages were unlike the others. They were divided almost exactly in half, with a front part and a back part. The front was where the lions, tigers, cheetahs, or panthers appeared before the public. The cages were lined up next to one another and as a whole they formed a single structure, one big block, with a little door on the side. The smell of meat, the scent of blood, reawakened the beasts and aroused them. And putting on an exhibition of that sort, it would seem, was not considered suitable. The keeper entered the little door and walked down the long corridor, stopping in front of each of the cages and tossing through the bars one, two, or three chunks of meat. Moussinac knew the appetite of each of his animals. For one of them twenty pounds of meat a day might not be enough, while for another five pounds was more than sufficient. Just as each animal's hunger was different, so was the manner of satisfying it, Monsieur Moussinac explained to Rembrandt. One might set aside its ration to consume it in solitude during the night, while another would pounce on it immediately, tearing into it until its teeth found no more bone, and then walk away. There were even some who pounced on a bone with their jaws, picked it clean, gnawed on it, licked it, and broke it into pieces to get to the marrow. But all of them, once they had finished their meal, assumed an expression of resigned, calm sadness.

One morning Rembrandt, having appeared early in the morning, as usual, before the gate to the zoo, found it closed. On that day no one was allowed in. "They're waiting for the gendarmes," Monsieur Moussinac explained. The night before, a man had hidden in the big warehouse where the zoo equipment was kept and waited until closing time. After dark he left his hiding place and, with the help of a ladder he found in the warehouse, he lowered himself into the bear's den. Maybe during the day he had seen someone toss a coin into the den. Maybe he had chosen that awful manner to end his days. Moussinac described to Rembrandt how he had discovered the man's body in the cage. He was lying on his back, with his chest ripped open from neck to belly. The ladder was still leaning against the wall of the den.

The bear, thought Rembrandt to himself, did not take advantage of that ladder to return to freedom.

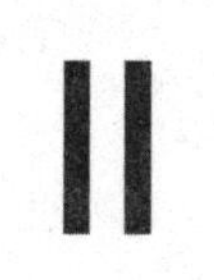

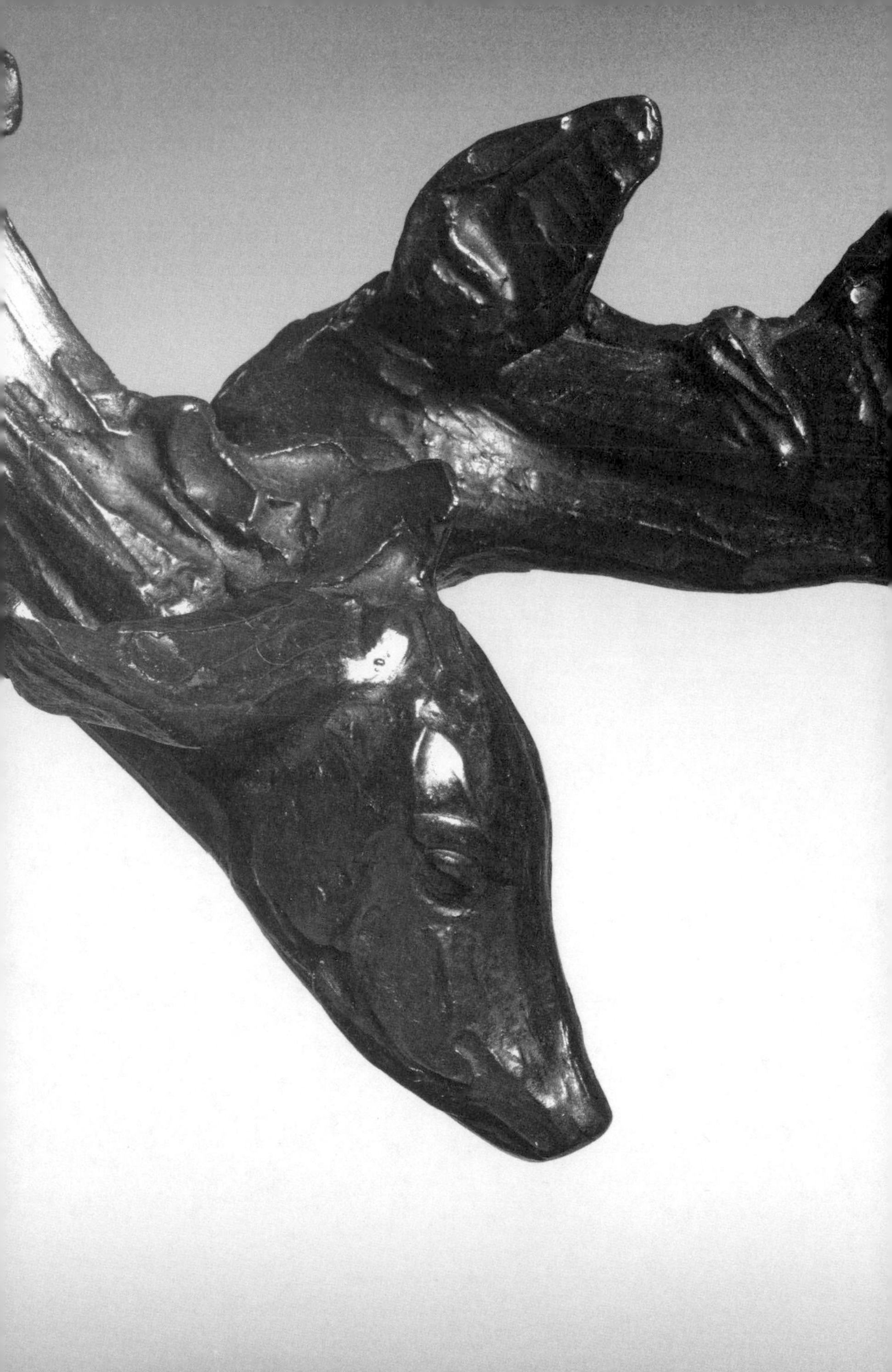

A blue enamel plaque affixed to the wall by the foot of the stairs indicated in white capital letters the availability of EAU & GAZ À TOUS LES ÉTAGES. Rembrandt Bugatti climbed the few steps that led to the mezzanine, the location of his lodgings, which also served as his studio. By that point Bugatti could consider himself satisfied with his artistic career. He had become a rather well known sculptor in France, Italy, and Belgium. But to do so he had had to overcome no small amount of misunderstanding, of skepticism.

The first obstacle had been the wishes of his father, who had envisioned a career as an engineer for him. As a railroad engineer, to be exact. There were already more than enough artists in the family. He changed his mind only on the day that he found, beneath a damp cloth in his studio, a terracotta group—a cowherd leading three cows—which Rembrandt, who was not even fifteen at the time, had modeled with his own hands.

And then there was the lack of enthusiasm shown by Adrien-Aurelién Hébrard, the owner of the art gallery on Rue Royale 8 and of the foundry where Bugatti had cast, by the lost wax method, the animals that he had modeled in Plasticine. According to Hébrard, it was the boy's last name that had intimidated him, since it evoked too much glory, too much art.

Nevertheless, journalists and critics began, as the years went by, to take notice of him and to consider, first with respect and then with admiration, the works he created. A few of them sensed the exceptional nature of the relationship between Rembrandt and his models. What distinguishes the talent of Monsieur Bugatti, they wrote, is his exact knowledge of the habits and behavior of animals: he seems to have lived with them, to understand their every movement and expression. Other critics boldly remarked that Rembrandt Bugatti loved animals not only as an artist, but also as a human being, with a love that verged on tenderness. It was therefore the man who helped the sculptor to grasp all the feelings that animals are able to manifest and to distinguish between their feelings—anger, affection, motherly love—as if they were human beings. If there was so much talk about him, they wrote, it was because the animals by this sculptor did not remotely resemble the efforts made by other artists thus far. And if one critic emphasized how in Bugatti there was a conscientious study of their flesh, a sharper perception of their skin, of their feathers, another would underline how it was thanks to his courage, his willpower, and also his patience that his achievement was there for all to see.

Rembrandt stood by the door. He slipped the key into the lock and went in. His portrait was hanging on a wall, inside a thin, dark, wooden frame. I have to decide whether or not to remove it, he thought.

The portrait was by André Taponier, the famous photographer. His atelier on Rue de la Paix had received not only some of the crowned heads of Europe but also a great many writers, artists, actors, politicians, and aristocrats, who would come to sit complacently for their portraits.

In the photograph, Rembrandt is dressed in his customary impeccable manner: a dark gray, double-breasted jacket with black silk trim on the cuffs and pocket flaps, a white shirt with a wing collar and the top buttons unbuttoned, a loosely knotted tie, and pearl-gray trousers. When he looked at the photograph Rembrandt could not help but think of Consul, the chimpanzee.

The story of Consul was a miserable affair that someone had related to him. It seemed that Consul used to go around wearing a tuxedo and donning a top hat on his head. He was well-mannered and elegant, ate and drank politely, patting his thick lips dry with a napkin that he would then replace on his knees. He had a small, graceful apartment with a furnished dining room, in the English style, as they say, a quite comfortable bedroom, and, finally, a bathroom with a chimpanzee-sized bathtub. They say that he had many interests but that the races were his greatest passion. Every year, on the first Saturday in June, he would attend the Epsom Derby, but without ever going so far as to wager a bet. A few years earlier, when the Olympic Games were held in London, the

Daily Mail had launched a fund-raising drive so the city could offer the best possible accommodations to the athletes, who were coming from every corner of the world. Consul did not fail to pledge his own support, sending in a check for one guinea, signed by his own hand.

At the Cirque Molier, in Passy, on the western outskirts of Paris, Bugatti witnessed something one night that gave him a sense of malaise and also great pain. It was a cross between a conference, an experiment, a demonstration, and what in the circus world is called a "number." (Bugatti didn't usually go to the circus, but this one time he made an exception.) Professor Pierre Hachet-Souplet, director of the Institut de Psychologie Zoologique, was at the podium.

The Institut's offices were near the Muséum d'Histoire Naturelle, which was located, like the zoo, inside the Jardin des Plantes. It is there that the professor normally held what he insisted on calling his "lessons." Sometimes, however, the halls of the Institut, which were small and dimly lit, were not big enough. More space was needed, as well as an actual ring. So Hachet-Souplet, together with his young assistants, moved to the circus. Not to the grand Cirque Medrano, but rather to the more discrete Molier.

Professor Hachet-Souplet had studied the Greek and Roman classics and published a few poems, as well as an essay on Stéphane Mallarmé. Then he started to study what he called "Techniques of Animal Faculties." To delve in deeper he wanted to learn in detail the practices adopted by professional trainers. He reached the conclusion that "in general, the better trained an animal is, the freer it is." In his opinion, every action learned during taming pivoted on hunger and fear, or on both at the same time: to allow the trainer to come close, the animal has to know the desire and the need to eat food; to take its distance from the whip, it must know pain.

One day Rembrandt came across an issue of the quarterly bulletin published by the Institut de Pyschologie Zoologique. It featured two studies by Professor Hachet-Souplet. The first was titled, "Animals in Front of the Mirror": a half dozen pages, complete with illustrations, in which the professor explained that all mammals, large and small, require training in order to recognize themselves in a mirror. The director of the Institut gave the example of an old lioness that, seeing its image reflected in a mirror, became ferocious, bared its teeth in anger, and started to roar. It was only after a few attempts—"forty-five," to be exact—that it managed to recognize itself. Similar experiments—"all with the same encouraging result"—had been conducted at the Institut's laboratories on other animals—a bear, a tapir, a young zebra—and also on some birds: night herons, egrets, and pigeons. Although, with regard to this last species, the professor had to admit in all honesty that, "they take time to recognize themselves, and even then I'm not so sure that they do."

In the longer and more detailed study, Hachet-Souplet returned to the more general question of training and focused his attention on the "trainer's voice." He wrote that in training, the voice, and in particular its tone, played a very important "impulsive or moderating" role. During the training sessions, the voice has to go through a whole range of intonations, "from cheerful encouragement to loud cavernous shouts." According to the professor the various nuances of tone had to be applied wisely: the voice served, depending on the occasion, to caress or to castigate. And particular attention should be paid to pronouncing and articulating words very clearly: "Commands must be short," he concluded, "it's useless to attempt long conversations with animals."

So one afternoon, Bugatti decided to attend one of these conferences, or rather lectures, that Hachet-Souplet gave at the Cirque Molier at irregular intervals, but at a minimum of two or three times a year.

The Molier had a small, covered riding ring inside a sturdy, luxurious building with wood plank floors and globe lights which hung from the ceiling. The gallery ran all along the walls and had a parapet with short thin columns making it look more like the balustrade of a terrace or an Andalusian balcony than the bleachers of a circus. The ring was surrounded by a raised divider covered in red velvet, like a sofa. Rembrandt found a seat among the public, in the first-floor gallery, close to the back row. On his face he wore the tense and restless expression that only a state of physical indisposition or apprehension could create.

A few days later Rembrandt would give his brother Ettore a desolate description of what he had witnessed that afternoon.

"It was nauseating," he said, "a disgrace!"

Ettore was the only person whose advice Rembrandt sought, and the only one in whom he regularly confided.

"A truly abject spectacle," continued Rembrandt. "Ernest Molier, the owner of the circus, appeared in the ring and announced that Professor Hachet-Souplet would be arriving shortly. Before he came on two acrobats performed, dancing and doing a high-wire routine. Molier, in order to introduce the number or maybe only to buy some time and allow the professor and his students to complete all the preparations for their performance, took the floor, entertaining the audience with a speech on the intelligence of animals. From ants to monkeys. The usual stories. In his comments on ants, he brought up Montaigne, who had frequently, he claimed, praised their amazing organizational abilities. He started to cite, one by one, lizards, ostriches, bears, bees, elephants (mainly to assert that the notions of big and little are not absolute concepts, but have meaning only in relationship to humans) and fleas, in which he saw not only the gift of intelligence, but also the capacity to employ, when the need arose, an incredible muscular force. Then he expounded on the behavior of spiders, celebrating what he called their magnificent and mysterious webs; ended his disquisition by mentioning crows and their ability to mimic the sounds of dogs, roosters, and tree frogs, the patriarchal habits of mice and their vivid, penetrating gaze, and concluded, finally, with an encomium of cats, which can open closet doors by themselves. After which he invited the professor to come to the ring. Hachet-Souplet arrived, made a bow of sorts, thanked Molier for the opportunity being granted to him once again, and also ventured to say a few words before beginning his number. A few words that sounded to me almost like a defense, though uttered in a haughty and peremptory tone. 'Training,' he shouted, addressing the audience, 'is a systematic, total fight against laziness. The idea of taming might not be agreeable to those who are almost hypnotized by the word freedom, the tamers of the sentimental school, shall we call it that, but the truth is that, as a rule, the better trained animals are, the freer they are, while if it were up to them, they would exert the least muscular and mental effort.' He went on to conclude that, 'Excellent training cannot but include, inevitably, excellent discipline.'"

Ettore listened to Rembrandt's story, nodding distractedly and without comment. Anyway his thoughts, for a few months now, had been focused mainly on the "Hermès vehicle," a prototype that carried a four-cylinder engine with a 140mm cylinder bore and a 160mm stroke, two valves per cylinder and the camshaft in the front.

He couldn't shake the idea, which he talked about—as a journalist from the *Gazzetta dello Sport* wrote—with such enthusiasm that he already seemed to be going sixty miles an hour.

The only animals my brother is interested in are steam horses, Rembrandt once remarked, more resigned than displeased, in one of the only witty remarks that ever escaped his lips.

"After that Hachet-Souplet called his assistant," Rembrandt continued his story, "and I was stuck watching first a rabbit playing the drums, and then a kangaroo, or maybe a bear, riding a tricycle. Nothing new. The audience applauded that travesty, of course. But the next scene was beyond the pale. From out of the darkness came another of the professor's assistants, bringing on a leash four animals that from a distance looked like dogs. In reality they were four jackals that jumped rope, walked upright on their hind legs, and in the end danced the waltz. It was disgusting, intolerable. I stood up and left."

A spectacle of this sort depressed Rembrandt. One day he listened to Foujita, a Japanese artist who lived in Paris and drew female nudes, still lifes, and cats, describing the miniature theaters in his country where trained birds would perform. Birds that play miniature musical instruments, Foujita assured him, fence with microscopic swords, ride on little wooden horses, walk a tightrope while holding a tiny umbrella in their beaks. Once I saw with my own eyes, in one of those theaters, a courtroom of canaries administering justice. The trial was for a canary accused of desertion. But the most extraordinary thing, he added, happened after the judges issued their sentence, the death penalty, while the canary deserter listened stiffly in his blue military-style frock coat: another canary wearing a miniature black hood appeared on the scene and executed him, cutting off his head!

IN HIS APARTMENT on Rue Joseph-Bara, Rembrandt did not have a single pet. Not a dog, not a cat, not even a bird. Perhaps he could no longer bear the sight of human beings and animals living in close confinement. Years before, when he had just arrived in Paris from Milan, he lived with his father and mother on Rue Jeanne-d'Arc and had his studio at a short distance, on Rue Duméril. On more than one occasion, on his way home, he chanced upon a little man taking a walk followed by a pack of dogs of every size and breed.

The man was Maurice Boissard, someone told him one day. He was the theater critic for the *Mercure de France* and lived on the Passage Stanislas, in a house filled with animals. Every night he would go out wearing a misshapen hat on his head and a filthy overcoat. He was taking his dogs out to do their business. And he often spoke with them.

One night Bugatti witnessed a fight between Boissard and a passerby. One of his dogs must have bitten the man's leg. The man started screaming, cursing and complaining about the pain. The critic from the *Mercure de France*, when Bugatti approached, also started to shout and to hurl abuse. "You, sir, are a peasant and a lout!" he said, looking at Rembrandt for approval.

THE ONLY ANIMALS that did share Rembrandt's studio on Rue Duméril for a few months were two small antelopes from Senegal, a male and a female. They were sent to him one day by Michel L'Hoëst, the director of the Antwerp zoo, entrusting them to his care. It's not that there were no antelopes at the Jardin des Plantes. It's that Rembrandt wanted to work particularly on the two animals he had gotten to know in Antwerp and whose life behind bars he had long observed.

"They'll stay with me for a little while," he told his mother, "they're just a little bit bigger than a dog."

Madame Bugatti bent down, her nose almost touching the fur on the back of one of the antelopes. "But they have a nauseating smell," she said, then added, "Well, if it makes you happy."

With a few light taps on their necks, Rembrandt drove the two animals up the stairs. That same night he started working on the antelopes. No preliminary sketches, no rough outlines on paper. As was his custom. Rembrandt observed them, observed them a second time, and then observed them again. But this time there were no cages, there were no bars. He watched them roaming around the studio, sniffing in the corners, licking the few sticks of furniture, chewing at the stuffing of an old sofa, beating their hooves on the floor. He contemplated them while they nibbled on the lettuce leaves, small green apples, corncobs, and carrots that filled the bathtub, which had been transformed into their trough. Rembrandt had also arranged some straw in a corner of the studio. They'll sleep on it, he thought. He called one of them simply "the little one," to distinguish her from the male, who was slightly bigger (Rembrandt didn't want to give them names, since he considered names one of those things that, in the relationship between man and animal, serves the useless purpose of humanizing the beasts). Well, the little one huddled in front of the door and, ever since that moment, fell asleep every night in that same spot. The two antelopes of Senegal would stay at Rue Duméril from June to September, after which they returned to their cage in Antwerp.

On September 27 Rembrandt wrote to Michel L'Hoëst: "Dear Sir, this morning I received a telegram in which I was informed that the two dear animals have arrived safely. I am certain you will excuse me for having done everything in such a hurry: but I had to take advantage of a quarter hour of energy before I could decide to separate myself from them. After so many months of living together, they had become true companions of my life and my work." Then, with the care of a parent and the delicacy of a lover, he added, "You will undoubtedly have noticed that the male is fatter and his fur has become darker. He's a superb animal . . . I hope the trip didn't tire them out too much. If you could write to me that they're alright, I would greatly appreciate it . . ."

Maurice Boissard, the *Mercure de France* theater critic, stopped Rembrandt Bugatti on the street one day.

"I hear you are interested in demonstrations of animal intelligence," he told him. "You should meet my friend Remy de Gourmont, who has been studying thinking animals for some time now."

This is a decidedly fashionable subject, thought Bugatti to himself.

"It's odd," Boissard continued, "I always thought Remy was looking at the animals only as animals, beautiful or ugly, pleasant or unpleasant, for companionship. Not like his brother Jean, whom I also know. Jean always speaks so tenderly about his cat, Zigoui, and how the little beast places its paws on his chest and with little darts of its tongue caresses his cheeks. But I was wrong about Remy. Stop by to see him. He doesn't get out much, lupus has been devouring his face for a few years now."

Bugatti had already run into Remy de Gourmont once at the Jardin des Plantes. The writer was sitting on a park bench and observing a lemur from Madagascar behind bars. Although he covered his face with his hands or with a large kerchief that he kept taking out of his pocket and putting back, Bugatti recognized him. In Paris there was a lot of gossip about the lupus that had corroded his facial skin and almost completely destroyed his nose.

Bugatti, as we know, was nothing if not annoyed by the idea of thinking animals and all the talk about the topic but, a few days later, he climbed the wooden stairs that led to the small apartment on Rue des Saints-Pères where Remy de Gourmont lived, surrounded by books.

"I almost never go out anymore," said Gourmont, who was wearing a dressing gown very similar to a cassock. "You understand me. I go by myself, every now and then, to the editorial office of the *Mercure de France* or to the Jardin des Plantes."

"I saw you there one day," Bugatti said, "in front of the cage of a lemur from Madagascar."

"What a beautiful animal, with its black and white fur," Gourmont said, in a shy voice with a slight stutter. "Luckily man invented the art of apparel," he added, looking at Rembrandt, who that day was wearing a light brown, flannel corduroy jacket with two long parallel rows of buttons, black trousers, and a necktie knotted with at least six loops. Gourmont continued. "Naked, man would have cut a rather sad figure in proximity to nature, which has such harmonious forms and colors. The Greeks understood this, and to give the human form an honorable status by comparison to the animal, they shaved the hair from their arms, legs, and chests and rubbed oil over their bodies, giving them a shiny patina."

Gourmont, whom his friends called *l'Ours*—the Bear—was sitting in a wicker armchair, behind a desk piled high with papers and books. In his hand he held a pair of pince-nez eyeglasses.

"Knowledge of animals," he said after a moment of silence, "is in my opinion the necessary premise to knowledge of man."

Rembrandt did not agree with Gourmont's statement, but he said nothing. Nor did he feel like responding to a subsequent consideration by the writer, which he could absolutely not share, namely that the wonders of animal intelligence are the progressive result of nothing more than long practice.

"It is no longer possible to doubt what Zarif and Muhamed are doing. These are facts attested to by men of science," said Gourmont. "They answer every question posed to them by shaking their heads or nodding, depending on whether they want to say yes or no. I am thinking of Elberfeld's horses. The literature is already vast," explained Gourmont. "They can do addition, subtraction, multiplication, and even extractions of square roots. They give their answers by tapping their hooves. To say sixty-two they tap six times with their left hoof and two with their right. Someone should make up their mind to sculpt one of those horses, by going to the lessons of Master von Osten, the trainer of thinking horses. Emmanuel Frémiet, for example, if you really don't want to do it yourself! Rather than an animal sculptor, Emmanuel is basically a horse sculptor." Gourmont continued. "Yes, of course, he does occasionally sculpt a cat, a dog, or an orangutan, but he sculpts horses more than any other animal. Warhorses, parade horses, but in particular bronze horses that are more appropriate to a veterinary institute than to a museum: dying horses, I mean to say."

Emmanuel Frémiet taught animal drawing at the Muséum d'Histoire Naturelle of Paris and Bugatti attended some of his lessons in his spare time, but without much enthusiasm.

"You know, I imagine, the source of his interest," said Gourmont. "As a boy Emmanuel worked at the morgue, painting corpses. In the sense that after maybe reconstructing a body decapitated by blows of a hatchet, or sliced up by a mowing machine, he would dab a little color on the lips, on the cheeks, on the forehead, or arrange the hair."

This must be the reason, Rembrandt thought to himself, that every time I see something by him, whether or not it's a horse, I always have the unpleasant impression that Frémiet sculpts with the unacceptable certainty, the idiotic presumption, that nature is revealing its most incredible secrets to him.

"Getting back to Elberfeld's horses," Gourmont continued, "they thought it might be remote transmission of thought, electric transmission. A scientific committee was appointed . . ."

All this talk about thinking horses left Rembrandt indifferent. He barely listened. He stirred only when Gourmont mentioned his "deer fly." They had shipped it to him from the Pyrenees, together with a sprig of heather, and it got its name—the "deer fly"—because of its exceptional but inoffensive horns.

"I put it in a display case, where it stared at the wooden columns, which were supposed to remind it of its native trees. It was waiting patiently for the tree to secrete the nectar on which the fly fed. Then I came up with the idea of feeding it with peach peels soaked in sugar, which it enjoyed, and it survived for the short life-span of the deer fly, just a few nights. But what a masterpiece of mechanical construction, what colors!"

REMBRANDT WAS STANDING in front of the cage of the Hamadryas baboon. He had been observing it for a while. He realized—or at least this was his impression—that for a few days now the baboon had been subjecting its every contemplated action to a torturous examination. Whether or not to enter its den, a kind of small cave built in the back of the cage. Whether to climb up or down a steel pole that was hung in midair across the entire length of the cage. Rembrandt watched it staring at its reflection in a small puddle on which strands of hay and a few tufts of fur were floating. It seemed to be using its eyes to look for its eyes. A gust of wind sent ripples across the surface of the water and together with the water a ripple went through the eye of the baboon and with that eye a thought. Then eye and thought came to rest on the dark bottom of the puddle and became illegible.

...

AFTER ANIMALS, REMBRANDT Bugatti's second favorite subject was himself. Nothing so strange about that. There was no denying that he had always taken great care and had great regard, an almost smug admiration, some whispered, for his appearance.

Bugatti did his self-portraits with pencil, graphite point (for the poster of his solo exhibit, *Exposition des Oeuvres*, at Antwerp's Société Royale de Zoologie in 1910), colored pencil and charcoal. He sketched quick, nervous images of his body and face on the back of postcards that he sent to his parents, brother, and sister, or to his *bon copain* André Taponier (with his head between the jaws of a lioness, or as a creature with elongated limbs, half-man and half-animal, or as a giant sculpting a tiny horse, or yet again with a face that has no eyes, no nose, and no mouth, hidden beneath a sombrero, in what he called "my brainless portrait").

Although in the opinion of some, the most sincere, most credible self-portrait Bugatti ever did was the one in which he used as his model the Hamadryas baboon of the Antwerp zoo (the same work that many consider his absolute masterpiece), he personally preferred the one in which he depicted himself with the features of a marabou. "I resemble a marabou," he wrote in a page of his notebook that conserves, in all probability, the rough draft of a letter. Like a marabou, in effect, he had long thin legs, a neck hunched forward, and a guarded style of walking. Wary.

When he was not doing his own portrait, Rembrandt had his friends do it for him. He posed for a plaster bust by Troubetzkoy (we will get back to this sculptor prince shortly), an oil portrait by Max Kahn, an etching by Walter Vaes, and two sculptures by Kathleen Bruce. In one of these last two, Rembrandt is nude.

"And to think that, the minute I arrived in Paris from London," Kathleen told him, "I used to flee at the sight of the nude models at the Académie Colarossi and lock myself in the bathroom."

Rembrandt spent long mornings in Kathleen's studio. Posing. Kathleen complained because she could never quite grasp his look. From one moment to the next, Rembrandt shifted from being a snob to being a shy, skinny boy (but one day she saw him lift a piano by himself), a serious, reserved man, a melancholic marionette.

Rembrandt, in turn, depicted Kathleen in bronze, but he placed a cat next to her. Kathleen told him that she had met Auguste Rodin and that she had been in his studio at the *Dépôt des Marbres*, where the Ministry of Public Works stored marble on Rue de l'Université. While she was waiting to be received (from the next room she could hear the loud, imperious voice of Rodin, issuing orders to his assistants), she opened one of the drawers of a giant credenza that occupied a whole wall. Then she opened another, and then another. "They all contained the same thing," she said. "Dozens and dozens of plaster casts of hands, of feet."

Rembrandt had also met Rodin, a few years earlier. But how could the two of them relate to one another?

One man spent hours and hours at the Louvre, as if he were listening to a long concert of beautiful music, where he would feel exhilarated, ecstatic, and find stimulation for his work. The other confessed that his only consolation was spending the whole day at the zoo.

One man challenged everybody: "I dare you to tell me that I've made an error, a single mistake in my anatomy!" The other admitted, without pride, without arrogance, that he completely ignored the anatomy of his models and trusted only in the precision of his eyes.

For one man, art demanded patience, perseverance, and he commented, "When you work, progress is slow, uncertain." The other sculpted quickly, decisively, and without hesitation.

Nevertheless, when the old sculptor with the face of a faun saw Bugatti's animals, he expressed words of admiration for him. There was one thing on which they could agree. Rodin also refused to force the models of his sculptures to sit for endless poses. Sittings, he said, are too laborious, premeditated, artificial, mannered. He proclaimed that he wanted to unite every aspect of a figure in a single sitting.

As for Rembrandt, what he liked observing in his models was precisely their movement, and certainly not static poses. How they crouched down, bodies extended, mouths half-open, claws unfurled. How lithely they arched their backs. How they shook their horns and beat their hooves on the ground. How they thrashed, twisted and turned when something caused them pain. He was fascinated to watch a tapir throw itself on the ground, tremble with fear, expel excrement. Or a fawn that stretched out on its back and rolled from side to side, opening and closing its jaws. Or a guanaco that spit out disgusting bubbles of spit. Or a monkey that liked to scratch its balls. Sometimes, after looking around himself to make sure no one was watching, he even tried to imitate the gait of the animals. He lifted his legs, moved his arms, shook his torso.

Movement is one of the questions that most obsessed him. (He wasn't the only one in his family with an obsession: his brother, Ettore, had a fixation on speed, the most extreme and exasperating form of movement, while his grandfather Giovanni Luigi racked his brains out, almost losing his mind, over the phenomenon of perpetual motion, another excessive, almost implausible aspect of movement). Rembrandt plumbed the depths of the problem. And he did not limit himself to observing incessantly the movements of his models. Instead he addressed the question with a more systematic method. One day he drew a dog with a skinny profile, subdivided the figure into four parts (front legs, rear legs, body, and head), and then glued it all to a piece of yellow cardboard and named his work *The Mechanical Greyhound.*

In this manner, he believed, he could clarify the physical, dynamic laws that govern the movements of a body. Nor would the architecture of the skeleton and the functions of its joints withhold their mystery from him any longer.

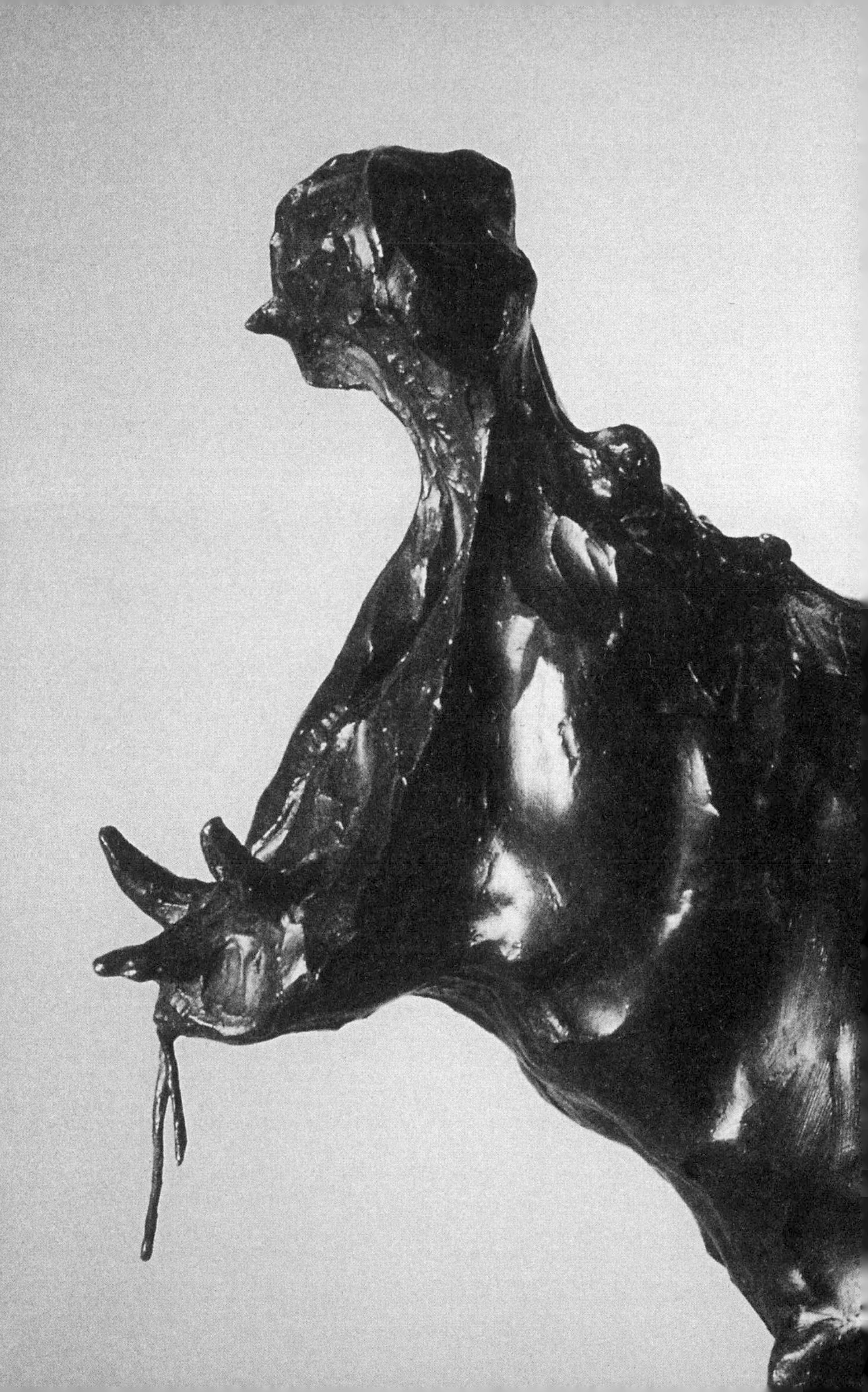

One Sunday in the summer of 1908, after long contemplation and having rejected the idea repeatedly, Rembrandt climbed on board the tram that departed from the Montparnasse station in the direction of the Bois de Boulogne. It was already late afternoon when he got off at the Boulevard Maillot stop. He started walking with long strides toward the side of the Bois de Boulogne that from Porte des Sablons leads to Port de Neuilly—to the exact location of the Jardin Zoologique d'Acclimation.

For the whole ride, Rembrandt had read a guidebook that he now pondered while heading toward the entrance to the zoo: the Jardin had been opened to the public "to introduce into France, by agreement with and under the direction of the Société d'Acclimation, every possible species of animal or plant, whether domestic or wild, for the purpose of intensifying their reproduction and educating the public."

After passing through the gate, Rembrandt walked down the main boulevard with a specific goal in mind. He was not interested in the big greenhouse on the left, which gathered every variety of camellia along with tropical flowers and exotic trees. Nor did the building located immediately after the greenhouse, where silkworms were raised, spark his curiosity enough to persuade him to make a short visit. And then what sadness, what revulsion, to see that halfway down the boulevard, Madame Odile Martin's *Grande Épinette Tournante*—the Great Revolving Chicken Coop—was still in operation. It was an enormous rotating cylinder divided into cells holding about fifty brooding hens. A man would feed them one by one, going up and down on a kind of hoist on a track: he would insert a rubber straw into the birds' beaks, press down hard on a pedal, and send the food directly into their stomachs. Many visitors to the Jardin would stop to observe, as if they were watching a show.

Rembrandt continued on, passing alongside an iron and brick tower more than one hundred feet tall, from which you could hear the cooing of an incalculable number of pigeon couples. He made it to the end of the boulevard and started to notice the first plaster and lime boulders, the winding brooks fed by the Paris city aqueduct, the little waterfalls that gushed from artificial ridges. There in the middle was a chamois climbing up a cement peak.

Coming toward him was old Juliette, the elephant who had survived by several years the death of her companion, Roméo. The two animals, he had heard, were a gift from Vittorio Emanuele II, the King of Italy, to replace Castor and Pollux, the two exemplars of the African elephant that the Jardin, in the siege of Paris during the Franco-Prussian war, had sacrificed to the hunger of the Parisians.

On her back Juliette was carrying a howdah upholstered in red fabric with silver fringes. Maybe it was just a coincidence, but as soon as she saw Rembrandt, Juliette raised her proboscis and trumpeted. The tremor made the two women and man in the howdah lose their balance, and they were almost thrown to the ground. One of the women screeched. So did an eagle in a cage.

An eagle screeches and everything in my mind becomes clearer, thought Rembrandt. Where did I read that? Or was it a bear growling, or a parrot squawking?

While mulling over these thoughts, Rembrandt continued without stopping until he neared his goal, at the edge of a fenced-in area. He did not get there alone, but was accompanied by a noisy swarm of visitors headed in the same direction. A crowd of feathered hats, straw boaters, kepi, bowlers, homburgs, and caps pressed together before the iron bars of a fence, but his height allowed Rembrandt to see the attraction that was drawing people from Paris and all France. (Rembrandt's height often made him look very frail, but being a head taller than people who reach your chest or shoulders also has its advantages.) There's no reason to hide the fact: Bugatti had been drawn to the Jardin d'Acclimatation by the same attraction, though for different reasons, driven by a desire that the other visitors might not understand. Combining the attention of his eyes with the attention of his mind, as he always did when he was studying his models, Rembrandt started to observe the forty Galla (he counted them immediately: there were twenty-five men, six women, and nine children) who had arrived from the highlands of Ethiopia. In previous years the Jardin had also exhibited, for the pleasure of its visitors, Lapps, Nubians, Eskimos, Kalmyks, Redskins, Caribs, Hottentots, and Bushmen. This time it was the turn of the inhabitants of the area of Africa lying between the Jubba River, Lake Rudolph, and Mount Kenya.

Without having to crane his neck or stand on tiptoe, Rembrandt contemplated both the vision of the whole and every minute detail of the spectacle, which had been staged for several weeks with supercilious care on a dusty clearing lined by a few gray trees. The other viewers were attracted by the Galla's attire: white cotton tunics that reached halfway down the leg or to their feet. They gazed with interest at the coral or amber necklaces, the earrings, the bracelets they wore around their wrists and elbows. The women's eyelids painted blue, the ivory combs in their hair. The men's shields made from antelope hides, their spears. The straw baskets they wove while squatting on their heels. Their games (they would toss a hoop into the air and try to stop its descent with an arrow). The crowd observed the dances performed in front of the mud and thatch huts, listened to the songs sung to the rhythm of copper sistrums. They offered them sweets and cigarettes. They admired the witch doctor, who had a panther skin draped over his shoulders and an ostrich feather in his hair. They sniffed in the air the pungent odor of the spices used to season peas and fava beans.

Rembrandt instead had eyes only for their bodies, so elegant and full of vigor. Their shoulders and arms, solid, strong, powerful. The slender legs with almost no calves. The high foreheads and thick, pink lips. The hair shiny with ox tallow. The long curly locks, with red tips, that tumbled to their shoulders. The braids from their foreheads or temples that ended at their necks, or that crossed the top of their heads, from one ear to the other.

When all the other visitors started to disappear, slowly but surely, because night was falling and the gates to the Jardin were about to close, slightly disappointed at not having arrived in time to see the Galla feasting on raw meat, painting their faces with animal blood, and flaunting the intestines as if they were necklaces, Rembrandt got even closer to the fence. The stench of ox tallow blended with the odor of cigarette smoke that one of them was inhaling with deep breaths, avidly, uninterruptedly. One more step. Now he could look them in the eyes. The setting sun brought out the fire and glow in the faces of the Galla, who took on the aspect of mysterious idols. A man with a dark beard covering his chin and cheeks raised his arm, stuck the spear he was holding between the bars, and shouting something, pointed it at Rembrandt.

"Get away from there, monsieur," warned a keeper who had come up behind him. "It's strange, but it's only when the public leaves that they become restless. Please make your way to the exit."

...

Ever since Paolo Troubetzkoy had arrived in Paris after a nine-year sojourn in Moscow, during which he taught at the Imperial Academy of Fine Arts, Rembrandt often dropped by to see him in his studio on Rue Weber. Roaming around the studio, free and undisturbed, there was a wolf, whom the prince called Vaska, and a fox. It was his penchant, and indeed it seems that in his Moscow studio he had also kept a bear and a horse, if we are to credit the word of Aleksandra Lvovna Tolstaya, who knew the artist well because he had executed three sculptures in bronze and a portrait in oils of her father, Count Lev Nikolayevich Tolstoy. Troubetzkoy—who had known Bugatti as a child, encouraged him and played an important part in his artistic formation—admired the Italian's work.

"When I see certain things, certain statues with eyes like egg yolks," he confided, "I become enraged. The first work that I did, at the age of eight, was of two deer. A marble bas-relief of two animals that we had in our garden at home."

The yellowish-brown snout of Vaska poked out from behind a damp cloth that may have been covering a block of clay. The wolf opened its mouth wide, emitted a low, dark sound, a kind of stealthy barking, came close to Rembrandt, and sniffed at him.

"Animals and their enigmatic stupidity," commented Troubetzkoy.

"Which is no worse than man's," observed Rembrandt.

"No, of course not," replied the prince, who later told his guest of his visit to the house of Robert de Montesquiou, for whom he had done a bronze portrait that was the talk of Paris, where he had seen his famous tortoise. The same tortoise on which the count had encrusted a jeweled shell. "And there were bats everywhere you looked. Bat lamps, bat furniture, what idiocy . . ."

For a period Rembrandt forgot about the zoo and its animals. Troubetzkoy opened up the Paris salons for him. He took him along to the most elegant parties, the most elaborate masked balls. To the *Fête Orientale* of Blanche de Clermont-Tonnerre, to the *Bal des Mille et une Nuits* of Aynard de Chabrillan, to the *Sparte au Temps de Lycurgue* of Pauline Lemaitre. It was on one of these evenings that Rembrandt made the acquaintance of Marie Ernest Paul Boniface, Marquis of Castellane-Novejean, known familiarly as Boni.

When a few days later he ran into the marquis again at the Hôtel Ritz, he was welcomed with these words. "Can you believe the noise? It's like being in the parrot cage at the zoo." We don't know whether it was by pure chance or whether Troubetzkoy had advised Boni of Rembrandt's passions. We do know that the marquis had a request for the sculptor. "Would you be interested in doing my portrait? In bronze?" Rembrandt accepted immediately, without thinking twice.

It was the originality of the clothes Rembrandt was wearing that most impressed the Marquis of Castellane-Novejean. Boni was a dandy who had, so to say, abolished all whimsy from his style of dressing. In addition to the cream-colored jackets that he combined with crimson-colored ties, the only other color he wore was gray, in the two variants of pearl gray and charcoal gray. While he conversed, his ivory walking stick was always in motion. And he took pleasure in observing Rembrandt, who on that day was sporting an overcoat that was a cross between a coat and a cape, which his sister, Dejanice, had made for him, a white suit with a double-breasted vest, a shirt with a high collar up to his chin, a bow tie, and on his head a brown hat in smooth silk velvet. On the lapel of his jacket Rembrandt had pinned the red ribbon of the *Légion d'honneur*, which France had awarded him a few weeks earlier "for artistic merit," and that was conferred upon him by the Undersecretary of State for Fine Arts, Étienne Dujardin-Beaumetz, an untalented former painter of wartime and patriotic subjects—*La brigade de Lapasset brulânt ses drapeaux, La garnison quittant Belfort, Á la baïonnette, Le bataillon des Gravilliers, Salut à la victoire*—which had nevertheless paved the way to his political career.

"Olivier, we must celebrate," said Boni, summoning the maître. Then he started to speak about his collection, the one he had been forced to sell to pay off his creditors. The furniture, the porcelain, the books, the paintings.

• • •

The sittings began one week later, at Bugatti's studio. The Marquis of Castellane-Novejean wanted to be portrayed in boots and with a knee-length riding shirt cinched at the waist by a belt. Rembrandt modeled the clay, as was his custom, with rapid, secure blows of the thumb, without second thoughts. While he was posing, Boni talked about the racehorses he used to own. Sleeping Car had won major prizes. Then there were Effendi II, Bolide, and Balchis, but his favorite was Emerick, who took first place at Auteuil, in the Prix de Haies de Printemps.

"To choose a horse you need to have the same impeccable taste required for a work of art. You need to observe and at the same time to understand. A rare thing indeed," commented Boni.

"Please," said Rembrandt, who wasn't used to hearing his models chat and had always preferred draft horses to racehorses.

But the marquis continued. "At my Palais Rose, which I no longer own, I had them paint groups of animals under the vaults of the central staircase to symbolize the five continents: elephants for Asia, camels for Africa, horses for Europe, and I don't recall which animals for the other two continents. I've forgotten."

"But I have not forgotten," he continued, "the parties I threw at that perfect copy of the Petit Trianon of Marie

Antoinette. Two thousand guests, valets in purple livery, the orchestra playing the "Marche Henri IV." At my summer residence—I no longer have that, either—I had wanted to create a menagerie to gather the most beautiful exotic creatures: ostriches, leopards, and so on. Unfortunately my circumstances did not permit me to, but you would have loved it, I imagine."

IV

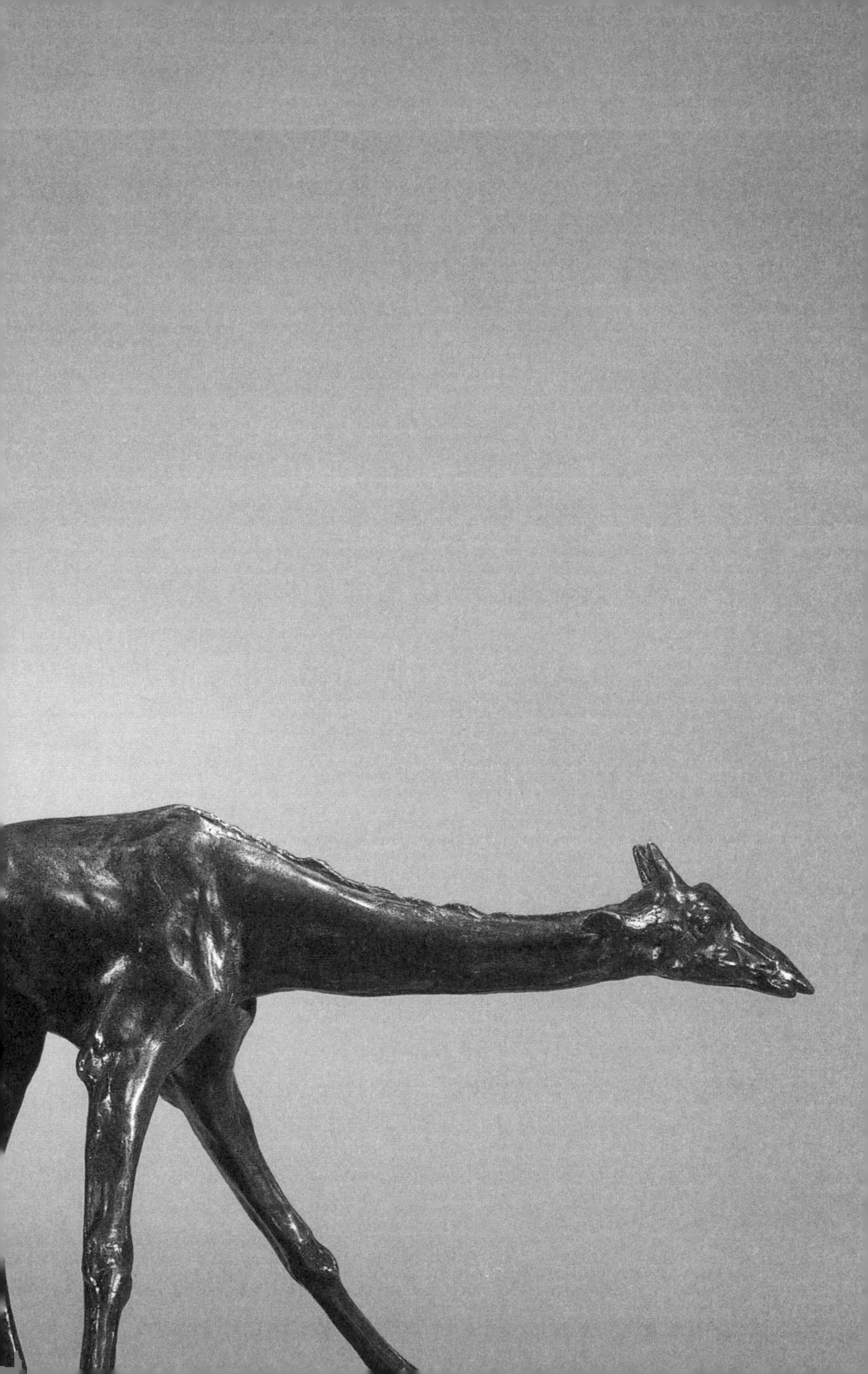

When he was in Paris, Bugatti could not imagine letting a single day go by without going to the Jardin des Plantes, and by the same token, when he resided in Antwerp, the days began de rigueur with a short walk from the house where he lived, on De Keyserlei, straight to the intersection with Van Schoonhovenstraat, and from there to Stationsplein, until he finally reached the city zoo, the place that fostered in him what he called his own "heritage of wildlife experiences." Rembrandt first set foot in Belgium in early fall 1906. "I have learned that an amazing rhinoceros has just arrived," is what he told his father, without further explanation, already prepared for his departure.

As soon as he descended from the train, and walked away from Antwerpen-Centraal, the large railway station of the Flemish city, he caught a glimpse, in the gray morning light, of the monumental white marble building of the zoo administration. Looking up he spied, with joy and the onset of vertigo, the colossal statue of a camel carrying a Bedouin on its hump, situated on the peak of one corner of the building.

Rembrandt didn't even bother looking for lodgings: with his suitcase in hand, beneath new volleys of rain, he went directly to the ticket office of the zoo. Waiting his turn in line, he looked impatiently at the two mosaics that decorated the entrance: a tiger fighting with a snake and a ferocious lion roaring with his mouth wide open. He purchased a ticket and entered, walking quickly and decisively down a wide avenue lined with chestnut and red beech trees.

To the left rose a building with large windows, topped by two domes: it was the Feestpaleis, the Festival Hall. To the right a lemon grove and, a little farther ahead, a wooden pavilion surrounded by streetlamps, chairs, and café tables, with stands for sheet music arranged in a circle under the canopy. A gust of wind blew over some of the music stands, and the rain started coming down in sheets. Rembrandt lugged his suitcase beneath the heavy raindrops that trickled under his shirt collar until he made it to a building with a vaguely Moorish façade: the Monkey House. The inside held giant cages in the back of which the dark silhouettes of several primates could be made out. The animals shook and shrieked, upset by the storm. One of them, a chimpanzee, broke away from the group. It approached the bars with its teeth bared and fur standing straight up on its back and neck, peeled its lips back and started to emit angry shrieks. Rembrandt looked at it for a moment and then headed back to the avenue. A few hundred feet away, he found himself before the great Egyptian Temple. With his trousers drenched up to his knees, he passed beneath the architrave, which was supported by four giant columns. On the two outermost columns the capitals were painted with date palm leaves, while the capitals on the two central columns were carved with the head of Hathor, the heavenly lady, the winged cow that gave life to creation. The frieze in the entablature told the story of the Temple in hieroglyphs. The ceiling of the vestibule was decorated on either side by rows of gold five-point stars against a blue field, connected down the middle by the outstretched wings of vultures. Rembrandt's eyes swept over the walls, covered with lions, ostriches, cheetahs, gazelles, giraffes, crocodiles, zebras, antelopes, hyenas, and leopards, together with the solemn figures of high priests, warriors, and the gods of the Nile. The mural depicted a world in which there is no defined hierarchy in creation, no hierarchy in which man occupies a position superior to other creatures. Or Rembrandt at least wanted to interpret it that way. Never before had he felt so close to understanding why one day he had confided to his brother the wish to consecrate all his time, all his energy, and all his qualities, conspicuous or insignificant though they might be, to the realization of works that no animal sculptor, ancient or modern, had ever succeeded in conceiving.

Inside the temple, in the vast, half-deserted, rectangular hall dominated by the skeleton of an elephant in the center, Rembrandt raised his eyes to the ceiling. Outside the rain had stopped and from above, through the windows of the large skylight looming over the room, a gray light descended that illuminated the elephant skeleton, lending it a ghostly appearance. The tusks in particular seemed to emit an incredibly vivid luminescence. Rembrandt cast a glance around. Behind the bars of the cages lining three sides of the hall he spotted the profiles of giraffes, camels, and zebras but, without hesitation, he headed toward the one in which the rhinoceros was enclosed.

The animal was in the back of the cage, sniffing at its own excrement. Its entire body was caked in a sort of dark dried mud.

To prepare himself for this encounter, Rembrandt had broken one of his own tenets, or rather, his rules. For the first time he felt the need to dedicate himself to a form of theoretical preparation. He sensed the need to master some general principles and considerations in the field of zoology. Zoology in the sense of the description and classification of animals, in terms of both comparative anatomy and the genetics of the species, in effect, which until then had never stirred any particular interest in him.

As a young man, in Milan, he had leafed through the *Historia animalium* of Aristotle, but he had been bored by the cataloging of six hundred animal species contemplated in that weighty volume. Later he chanced to browse, though again without any particular curiosity or emotion, the *Historiae animalium* of Conrad Gessner. Indeed, he had been quite frankly irritated by the fact that the Swiss naturalist in his interminable lists had inserted fantastic mythological animals. "I'm not going to waste any more time in this manner," he had promised himself.

The rhinoceros family includes four or five different species, between the Asiatic and the African branches, but in the antediluvian era there were many more—at least fourteen. These were the first notions that Rembrandt learned from the pages of the *Dizionario enciclopedico illustrato* published by Vallardi. And in the same book, which his father had brought with him from Italy, he learned that the Indian rhinoceros is distinguished by the fact that it has only one horn, and by its unpredictable but not ferocious temperament. Rembrandt also read the entry for "Rhinocéros" in the *Histoire Naturelle, générale et particulière* by the naturalist and cosmologist Georges-Louis Leclerc de Buffon, where he found confirmation that unicorn rhinoceroses are "neither ferocious nor carnivorous nor particularly savage," but that they are "nevertheless intractable . . . without intelligence or sentiment," and often "subject to fits of rage that nothing can calm." Buffon had observed two rhinoceroses in the flesh. The first, Clara, had been paraded through the fairs and courts of Europe for twenty years as a sideshow attraction. The second, the "Rhinoceros of Versailles," had been captured in Western Bengal, given as a gift to Louis XV, and died in 1793, a victim of the revolution, run through by a saber. Its embalmed body is kept at the Muséum d'Histoire Naturelle, and it was by studying it that Georges

Cuvier, paleontologist and continuer of the work of Buffon, was able to create the third work consulted by Rembrandt: *Observations anatomiques sur le rhinoceros.*

Once he had completed these readings, and felt that he had now learned enough, Bugatti left for Belgium with a firm grip on his newly-acquired knowledge.

After dragging its enormous mass from the point where its dung was collected all the way to the bars of the cage, the animal stopped in front of Rembrandt and looked at him, slowly opening its eyelids. Although he could touch it, if he extended his hand, and feel the warmth of its flesh beneath its crust of dirt and leathery skin, Bugatti thought it would be best, for the moment, to forgo such a gesture. As if awaiting a sign, a proof of attention, and irritated at not receiving one, or surprised by the man's apparent lack of interest, the pachyderm lowered its head to one side, rubbed it against the ground a few times, and then returned to its dung heap.

I have to speak with the man in charge here, thought Rembrandt as he left the Egyptian Temple.

Michel L'Hoëst, who was the director of the Antwerp Zoo (the L'Hoëst family was a dynasty of directors: first Michel François, followed by Michel Junior), welcomed him affably and courteously, without the prudent skepticism that in other circumstances he might have reserved for a man like Rembrandt: an Italian who was quite tall, although a little hunchbacked, with facial features that were melancholic and sharp, though not exactly severe, and dressed in a style that, at a minimum, could be described as subtly bizarre or strangely provocative.

"All animal sculptors are welcome here," said L'Hoëst, with a hint of pride in his voice. "For them our arms are always open! We do everything in our power to make them happy, to support their creative process."

Perhaps the esteem and reputation that Bugatti had started to enjoy in France had also reached the ears of the director.

The first visit, the first contact of Rembrandt with the Antwerp Zoo, was thus limited to a quick stroll through the Egyptian Temple, a brief stop before the Indian rhinoceros, and a meeting with L'Hoëst. But it was the beginning of a bond that would grow closer and stronger, and Bugatti's stays in Antwerp became longer and longer. Every time Rembrandt found himself in the Flemish city, he would visit the zoo on an almost daily basis. Even when, sometime later, he abandoned his room on the second floor of the De Keyserlei to go live, together with two other animal sculptors—Albéric Collin and Oscar Jespers—in a large studio on Begijnenvest that was cold, unhealthy, and reeking of mold, he did not let himself be discouraged by the distance. Nor would he disavow his "imperious, almost burning" desire—as he himself defined it—to reward his gaze with the vision of animal life that took place on the other side of the bars and fences of the Antwerp Zoo.

Every day, around midmorning, Rembrandt would appear before the gates of the zoo with a supply of modeling clay. (He prepared it himself, with clay, lard, and powdered sulfur; this composition made the material firm but never completely hard.) With a nod in the direction of the ticket booth, an exchange of greetings—*"Goedemorgen!" "Goedemorgen, heer Bugatti!"*—and on rare occasions a knowing smile, he would breach the entry, proceeding straight to the place at the center of his interest that particular day.

Sometimes it was the Monkey House, whose large cages seemed to swell by the day to accommodate as many exemplars as possible: chimpanzees, baboons, macaques, gibbons, Borneo orangutans, Liszt monkeys (so-called because of their white mane, similar to the composer's coiffure). Or else the wooden boxes with narrow doors in which the reindeer and antelopes lived, the meadow on which the yaks spent their days reclining, or the iron grill beyond which the tigers paced back and forth.

In the company of Albéric Collin and Oscar Jespers, Rembrandt often spent the late afternoon and evening seated at a table on the large terrace of the Hotel Weber. The three animal sculptors drank absinthe, played dominoes, and engaged in conversation. It was on these occasions that Rembrandt proved to be a little more loquacious than usual, at least until the second glass of absinthe or the third beer, after which he would retreat into impenetrable silence. Sometimes the director of the zoo, Michel L'Hoëst, would sit at their table. More often they would be joined by André Demaison, a man from Bordeaux who traveled widely. He had crossed Western Africa high and low and knew the Jola, Wolof, and Mandingo languages. He was short, stout, and had a toothbrush moustache topping an energetic mouth. Demaison captured exotic animals on behalf of the Antwerp Zoo. ("I'm a little like the first Christians, condemned to being surrounded by wild animals," was his favorite remark.) For some time now, although he had not completely forsaken his nets and rifles (if he had a vocation, it was indeed the hunt), he seemed to be attracted by a new type of prey.

It all began two years before, he said. One day I arrived in a village between Dakar and Guinea and they brought a boy to show me. Take him into your service, they said. He was half naked. He looked strong and robust. All he requires is a lot of food, they added. We don't know where he comes from. The women are afraid of him. He must have been fifteen or sixteen years old. One detail struck me in particular: he had arms that were much longer than normal. Then they confided in me that he had been raised by nonhumans, by leopards. I didn't want to believe them. Look at how he climbs trees, they continued, or how he runs, or the way that he rips apart and devours every chicken he sees on the roads of the village, and you'll see if we're not telling the truth. I ended up taking him with me, and until almost the last day I remained in Africa he was a member of my servitude. He was respectful, devoted. But he died when he jumped into a river and was devoured by a crocodile that I thought I had killed: he was trying to retrieve the body. A few months after my return to Europe, at the home of Doctor Chardère of Marseille, I saw another one of these creatures. Sylvie, as Chardère called her, had grown up amid a troop of apes. There was something not quite right, something dissonant in her brain, said Doctor Chardère, almost like an organ that had stopped working through long inactivity. Sylvie walked on bent knees and ankles, with the fingers of her hands scraping the ground. She rejected cooked food and did not want to wear clothes or shoes. She had a highly developed sense of smell and recognized people by their odor. The doctor told me that he had asked permission to place Sylvie face-to-face with the apes in the Marseille zoo to highlight their similarities and differences. The directors of the zoo finally granted permission and I accompanied him there. Chardère had her enter the cage but, after casting a look around, Sylvie huddled in a corner with her chin pressed against her knees, and from there she didn't budge, limiting herself to emitting occasional grunts, whether from fear or pleasure it is hard to know. As for the apes, two of them dared to approach her, but they took their distance immediately, maybe because something flashed in Sylvie's eyes for a moment that only Doctor Chardère had noticed. The doctor seemed deeply moved, so much so that he went to Sylvie and kissed her twice on the cheeks. In the meantime a small crowd had gathered in front of the cage, so Chardère illustrated his theory out loud: birds that come from Spain do not understand the chirping of those who live in France or in Italy or in Hungary, just as Sylvie and the apes in this zoo do not understand each other because they come from different countries. Since that day I have realized that it wouldn't be a bad idea to dedicate my travels and my explorations not only to hunting exotic animals but also to collecting wild children. So far fate has not smiled upon me, but I have no doubt that, sooner or later, I will chance to come across one of these phenomena again.

In the meantime, Demaison had studied the issue, and thanks to the help of Doctor Chardère he now had a decent mastery of the subject, which he flaunted tirelessly in his conversations with Bugatti, Collin, and Jespers, his artist friends. Indeed, for a while their evening conversations ended up being long monologues by the "hunter," monologues that the three animal sculptors listened to in silence, nodding and continuing to play dominoes or drink absinthe or beer, while the dying light of Antwerp gave off its last timid shots of artillery. Demaison told them about the wolf-child of Asia, the bear-boy found in the woods of Lithuania, or the calf-child of Bamberg who snarled and snapped in furious fights with dogs. The three young men gave no sign of wishing to contradict him.

Demaison spoke quietly, almost whispering, until something in his story excited him in a particular way, and then he became animated and suddenly raised his voice.

They were leaping—do you get it—from one rock to another, like two chamois, he said, when some hunters found them in a lost valley of the Pyrenees. Rousseau also talks about them in his book. In the beginning there was no way to make them stand still except by threatening them with a stick. Then they began to understand hand gestures and to respond to greetings. The King of Spain took their schooling to heart but, although over time they learned to do the most necessary things—eating, drinking, sleeping and so on—there was not, in truth, an appreciable change in their character or in their habits.

Every now and then Albéric Collin would interrupt Demaison, breaking into the conversation with a few words of mild teasing. Of the three animal sculptors sitting at the table in the Hotel Weber, Collin was the only one who could boast a more than passing knowledge of the classes, orders, families, genera, and species into which animals are subdivided. It is a quality that can be grasped in the scrupulousness, fidelity, and meticulous attention to detail with which he made his works (he went so far as to measure the length of the claws of lions, tigers, and panthers). Among the critics and simple habitués of art galleries there never failed to be someone who held this quality against him, criticizing him as a translator enslaved by and faithful to tangible reality.

"In short," said Collin one night, "all your 'savages' immediately demonstrate a positive attitude and a certain satisfaction over their new life, but deep down they never express any intolerance of or aversion to their past."

Demaison burst out in laughter. "Now don't get so threatening and insulting with me," he said, while his stomach shook.

Which threat or insult Demaison detected in Collin's words is not clear, nor did it become so when he added, "One can hear echoes of Rousseau in what you say. Or are you perhaps one of those who is moved to tears when you hear the story of Napoleon's bastard, Kaspar Hauser?"

One night it was Rembrandt who broke his customary silence and addressed Demaison in an unexpectedly vicious tone, telling him to his face that when he listened to his stories he had to struggle not to throw up. Then, as if to reinforce his words, he spit on the floor. On the pavement a clot of mucus formed that was streaked with threads of blood. With the tip of his shoe Rembrandt rubbed it into the ground.

After a while life in Antwerp began to nauseate him. From his current lodgings, on Begijnenvest, he could no longer see the zoo. The damp room that reeked of mold, and that doubled as his studio, filled him with distress. Sometimes, while he was walking down the streets of the city, returning from the zoo, he had the impression that he stank to high heavens, but the people, rather than turning their embarrassed gazes away and taking their distance, seemed to stare at him insistently and then come closer to sniff at him.

Only in his work, as he wrote in a letter to his sister-in-law, Barbara, Ettore's wife (with whom he may have once been in love), did he "find complete happiness." But he also confided in her, as if happiness were a crime, that he should never have become an animal sculptor. "I wrote to Ettore but he never wrote back. He must be in Le Mans," an assumption Rembrandt made, one is led to believe, because he had read about it in the newspapers. So he asked Barbara to please convey his congratulations to his brother on the "Peugeot Bébé."

In a letter some time later to "Totor"—the nickname Rembrandt used for his brother, who in turn called him "Pempa"—he thanked him for sending money, which allowed him to "buy some warm sweaters." He then added, "I have a touch of pleurisy, and two days ago I could hardly breathe. Now I'm feeling better." And he concluded, "Yet still this life weighs heavily on me."

One morning Rembrandt received a letter. The address printed in the upper right-hand corner of the envelope, in blue characters (first in Flemish, then in French), indicated the sender: the director of the Antwerp Zoo, Michel L'Hoëst.

Who knows why he's writing to me, thought Rembrandt, turning the envelope over and over in his hands without making up his mind to open it. Writing me when we already see each other almost every day at the zoo or at the Café de l'Union. Only at that point did it dawn on him that for the past week they hadn't had an occasion to meet.

Rembrandt opened the envelope. Inside was a card. One of those elegant cards that L'Hoëst usually wrote on Christmas to send the season's greetings. On one side there was a reproduction of an engraving of the Reptile House at the zoo: a kind of Hellenistic temple with a series of columns and gables in which snakes, crocodiles, iguanas and also tortoises and turtles were exhibited. On the other side these words were written: "My dear friend, the horrible but also, in some way, merciful carnage will take place tomorrow. While I have been spared the tremendous suffering of having to issue the command to open fire, I still have had, however, to scrupulously organize everything myself . . ."

Rembrandt read it and reread it, placed the card back inside the envelope, and then returned to take it out again and read it once more. The words looked to him like shiny black insects staring up at him, rubbing their legs together.

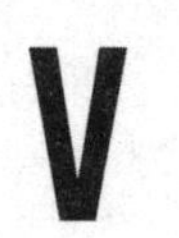

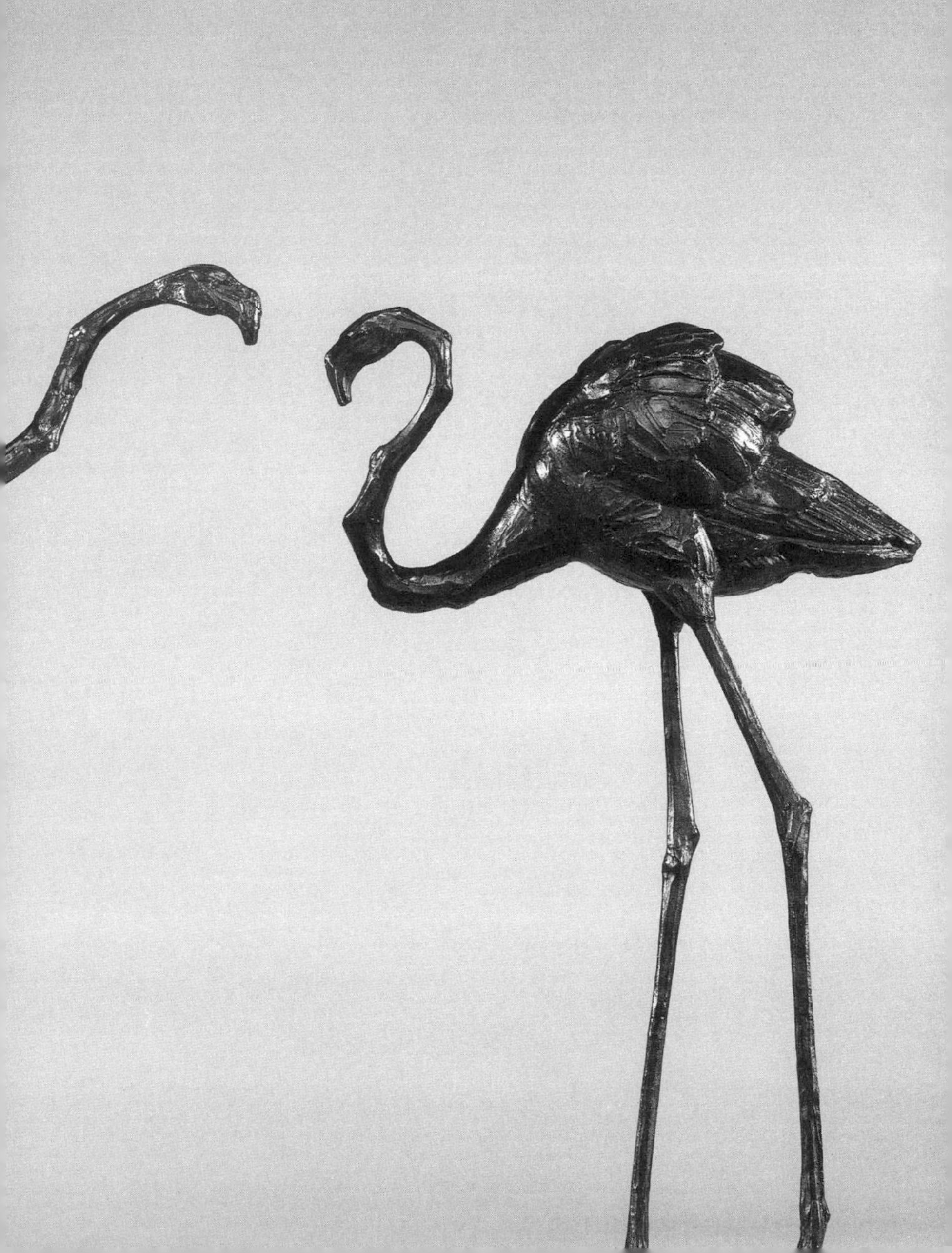

As of August 20, under the advance of the divisions of the Central Powers, the capital of Belgium was no longer Brussels but Antwerp. The Austrian 305-millimeter mortars and the 45-ton Krupp howitzers had devastated the cities and laid waste to the villages. Liège was overrun and torn asunder. The news that Rembrandt read in *Le Matin d'Anvers* was shocking. All was being submerged beneath a dark flood of atrocities, horrors, and perversions. The trees were gone from the countryside and the fields were burning. The roads were lined on either side with the bodies of the dead: decomposing corpses immersed in puddles of rain and blood. The houses had been looted. Chairs, armchairs, and mattresses had been gutted, furniture overturned, tiles ripped up, wallpaper torn off, in search of gold, jewelry, cash. Requisition orders were posted on walls riddled with gunfire but still standing. Bodies were hanging from telephone poles. The Germans had set fire to barns, pouring gas first on the pigs and the cows. The elderly had been forced to march at the head of columns of the imperial army of Wilhelm II, to act as human shields against the gunfire of their fellow citizens who were resisting the invasion. Those who didn't march fast enough on the muddy roads were rewarded with a bullet to the nape of the neck. Children were beaten to death with the butt end of rifles before their mothers' eyes. Sons and husbands were bayonetted before their sisters, their wives, who were then ordered to dig the graves. Girls were raped and murdered, their bodies left by the sides of the road, skirts upturned, bellies sliced open. Boys were beaten and hung by their scrotum. Husbands and wives were bound together with rope, back to back, straw stuffed into their trousers and under their skirts: an officer would approach them with a smile on his face and a cigarette in his hand, ready to set them on fire. Children were ordered to dance before the bodies of their parents, to dance and sing the old folk song: *Il pleut, il pleut, bergère*—It's raining, it's raining, little shepherd girl. The bell towers of churches were toppled out of fear they could be used by snipers.

Perhaps all of this was not in strict compliance with the laws of war and the international conventions signed by the Kaiser, but the strenuous Belgian resistance had ultimately exasperated the soldiers of the German Army.

ON THE NIGHT of August 24 and 25, 1914, shortly after midnight, when the citizens of Antwerp were already in bed or about to turn in, a steady, incessant humming erupted from the sky.

Rembrandt stuck his head out the window and had the impression that the air itself was vibrating. Looking up he could see in the incredibly luminous sky the outline of a

Zeppelin slowly approaching, headed toward the center of the city. The machine looked powerful, threatening, but also a little comical. It was shaped like an enormous cigar. All of a sudden something was shot from the belly of the Zeppelin that resembled a shiny sparkler. A second later an explosion made the rooftops shake, the chimneys crumble, and the walls crack. The first bomb fell on Beurstraat. Next to be hit were Albert von Barystraat, Schermersstraat, Justitiestraat, the Waag, the public weigh station, the Falconplein barracks. Ten explosions in a row that blazed the passage of the Zeppelin over the city. The bombs—adorned, according to reports, by an engraving of the face of Wilhelm II—opened holes in the paved and cobblestoned streets that were as deep as craters. Gas pipes exploded and water pipes broke. By the end the casualty count reached twelve dead and more than fifty wounded.

On the next night the citizens of Antwerp remained awake in their houses, making do with candlelight, going to bed fully clothed, or sitting in the dark on the stair landings. They were waiting for the Zeppelin to cross the sky again. But the enormous cigar did not reappear. It would come the next day or the day after that, was the common refrain as they peered at the sky. While waiting they could not remain inert, they had to take precautions. And so they marked with chalk the houses that had a cellar or an underground room that could provide shelter, where mattresses and food supplies could be arranged. In the courtyards they prepared buckets of water to extinguish fires.

But they also contemplated less immediate, less evident possibilities. For example, the zoo was located next to the train station—a sensitive target—and therefore there was a big risk that those bombs that fell with a hiss, leaving a filament of light in the sky, would free the animals. Then they would swarm the streets in packs. Sniffing at doors, defecating on the townhouse stairs, bathing in the fountains. Trying to climb up to the windows of the homes. Perching on the huge signs that boasted the quality of Kub bouillon cubes. Or else, if a bomb should strike the cages and slaughter the animals, their bodies would lay rotting in the sun, since no one doubted that soon, very soon, there would no longer be any way to bury people, much less animals. It was a question of public health. And also of public order! There was a danger that the marabou, ostriches, and leopards might come to the tables of the Café de l'Union, where the businessmen played dominoes, or make it as far as the banks of the Schelda to drink from its waters.

The zoo adopted of its own accord emergency measures for the most dangerous animals: the small cats were caged in the cellars of the Feestpaleis—the biggest building of the complex—while the larger ones were moved to the armored cages normally used for transportation. The bears instead were too cumbersome, so no better expedient was found than to kill them immediately by gunshot. The escape of the animals was not the only problem. Maybe they wanted to prevent the enemy from seizing the most prized animals, property of the most beautiful zoo in Europe, and transferring them to Germany as war booty. The fact remains that the provincial governor, Gaston van de Werve et de Schilde, ratified the order: all the animals of the zoo had to be destroyed, without further delay.

"Yesterday they communicated to me the resolution of the municipal council," wrote the director to Bugatti, "granting me forty-eight hours to prepare everything. At five o'clock tomorrow morning I have to open the gates of the zoo to a battalion of soldiers who will handle the appalling business."

AT FIRST THEY had thought of assigning the "appalling business" to the Garde Civique, then they changed their minds. The Garde did not have sufficient training. Above all it did not have sufficient equipment: its single-shot rifles were not up to the task. Therefore, what appeared at dawn before the gates of the zoo was a platoon of fifty men from the Second Regiment of the Chasseurs à Pied, armed with Mauser repeater rifles with fixed bayonets. The soldiers were in high uniform: double-breasted, dark green jackets with a yellow cordon affixed to the shoulder, gray trousers with a thin yellow stripe down the side, and a shako topped by a crest of black feathers. No white gloves, only because gloves did not ease the task of loading the rifle. So why sully the uniform they would have to put on a few days or a few hours later to repel the enemy assault?

The soldiers spread out over the great entrance boulevard in orderly rows. They marched past the pavilion where, in peacetime, on Sundays in the late spring and summer, a band played the waltz, the polka, the marches, and they passed by to the Moorish building where the monkeys were housed. "We'll save that for last," said the captain who commanded the platoon. Perhaps they resembled man too closely, and it seemed awful to begin with them.

So they began with the birds. The aviaries that housed them were opened cautiously to prevent any from escaping. In each aviary, which were tall and spacious, two soldiers entered, while another stood right outside. As soon as the parrots saw the soldiers inside their cage they started to shriek wildly, flapping their wings, jumping from one perch to another. The two peacocks, beaks extended, pounced on the chasseurs, who had probably never expected a similar reaction from animals with such a regal bearing, such a harmonious gait. The doves and turtledoves instead conserved, even at that moment, their natural elegance and lightness in flight. The soldiers cocked their rifles and started to shoot. Their comrades in arms who did not enter the aviaries remained on the avenue, in formation, waiting for the others to complete their assignment. The bullets pierced the metal netting of the aviary, and the birds took advantage to escape. But for every breach, every opening that they found, they also encountered the rifle of the soldier posted outside. "I don't want to hear any shouts," said the captain to his men. "I don't want to hear any cries of enthusiasm. And I don't want to hear any cursing." In fact the only sound that could be heard were the gunshots, the cries of the birds, and the beating of their beaks against the metal netting, as well as the noise of the occasional bowl or feeder rolling over or shattering. When not a single bird was left alive in the aviary, the soldiers who had done the shooting rejoined their comrades who had remained standing, rifles on their shoulders, lined up along the avenue. The captain gave the order to get into a new formation and the platoon resumed its march. From the cages arose shrieks, moans, and howls of agony that drowned out the rhythmic thud of the soldiers' footsteps. For the great Indian elephant an almost regulation execution was organized, with a dozen soldiers arranged in two rows, the first crouching and the second standing. A sergeant gave the order to take aim and fire. For the tiger, by contrast, all it took was a shot right between the eyes. And a single bullet was also enough for each of the fallow deer, gazelles, and zebras. On the antelopes they didn't waste a single bullet, making simple recourse to the bayonet. The firing squad was reassembled, however, for the rhinoceros, the giraffes, and the hippopotamuses. The agony of the rhinoceros lasted for hours after the concentrated gunfire had felled him.

The next morning crows circled in the pale autumn sky above the zoo. The smell of gunpowder stagnated in the air and blended with the stench of corpses that fermented and became putrid. Amid the haste no thought had been given to the reduced capacity of the zoo's crematorium, while the quantity of animals was infinite. Because of the wait the carcasses had to be piled up near the fence, and the smell of blood drew packs of stray dogs for days and days.

That night Rembrandt had a dream. He found himself at the entrance to the Snail Room, hunched over, his long legs cramped. The room dated back to a few years earlier and had been conceived and built by his father, Carlo. It was made of oak and similar to the shell of a snail both in color and, if you touched it with your fingers, the porousness of its surface. Walking with his back bent forward, Rembrandt climbed the steps of the spiral that led to the room. At the center of the room there was an oval table, covered with a tablecloth of fine yellow brocade, on which miniature tapirs, anteaters, marabou, and ostriches the size of sparrows were moving excitedly. Next to the table, on a chair carefully upholstered in pewter and vellum, Carlo Bugatti was seated. On a sofa, with her legs dangling over an armrest that ended with the head of a giant snail, Rembrandt's sister, Dejanice, was lying down. The snail head had crystal eyes.

I built all this for the sultan of Constantinople, said the father severely, but neither you nor your sister is willing to boil the glue that holds it together. In the meantime the little animals have multiplied and no longer occupy just the table: they're swarming onto the chairs, the sofa, and they're starting to invade the floor.

You who love animals and are loved by them in turn, order them to leave.

At that point Rembrandt woke up, got out of bed, and dragged himself to a corner of the room where there was a pitcher and a basin, and splashed generous handfuls of water onto his face. Then he started to cough. A dry cough that hurt his sides and made him feel like vomiting. In the end he spit up a thick, foaming substance, a kind of clot, and the water in the basin turned red.

For a few days, like a wounded animal, it seems appropriate to say, Bugatti wandered in the vicinity of the zoo, without summoning the courage to enter or even get too close. To go beyond a certain limit. He roamed the streets around Antwerpen-Centraal railway station with his temples throbbing and his head in a fog. The giant howitzers started to thunder in the morning, raising clouds of black smoke into the air. The Germans, people were saying, have doubled their contingent opposite the fortifications that surrounded the city. From the station square Rembrandt noticed a pair of chasseurs standing guard in front of the zoo.

What are they guarding? he wondered. What are they protecting?

Then he left, started to wander again, walking aimlessly down streets littered with shattered glass and chunks of plaster, coming across columns of soldiers moving from one neighborhood to another, and groups of families leaving their homes with bundles on their backs, bundles into which they had crammed their most prized possessions as best they could.

As soon as the darkness came, with shaky legs and heavy feet, Rembrandt headed toward his studio on Beginenvest, where he threw himself on his bed, exhausted, and fell asleep.

ONE MORNING, TOWARD the beginning of September, before the indifferent stares of the two chasseurs (it seemed that no one had bothered to relieve them), Bugatti mustered the strength to cross the threshold of the zoo, and to enter, not without some hesitation, the great boulevard that led, after a slight swerve to the left, to the front of the Feestpaleis. The spectacle that appeared before his eyes was not what he had expected. Rather than desolation and silence he found an ample movement of people coming and going, a frenzy of activity. A frenzy that may have been heartrending but was still a frenzy nevertheless.

The wide terrace balcony, the restaurant, the café, the billiards room, the winter garden of the Feestpaleis, and especially the sumptuous atrium with its marble floors and shiny chandeliers by which one entered the concert hall had been converted into a makeshift hospital for the wounded. Badly injured and suffering soldiers were arriving from the front every day, in addition to the people whom the hospital trains had already evacuated from the south and center of the country, from the now lost provinces of Liège, Namur, and Brabant. Strange that Rembrandt had noticed nothing, after hovering around the station for days, despite being in the grips of a mild form of somnambulism.

"Do you know how to dress an arm, stop a hemorrhage, or administer medicine?" they asked him.

"No," replied Rembrandt.

"You look young and strong: I'm sure you can handle the poles of a stretcher."

After an hour of intensive training, during which they instilled in him a few rudimentary notions about the transportation of the wounded, as well as how to monitor them (it's important, they explained, to protect the wounded from themselves, to prevent them from doing stupid things or, worse, from making any rash movements), Rembrandt entered the ranks of the DSTP, the *dispensés du service en temps de paix*, those exempted from military service during peacetime. The other stretcher-bearers were mainly teachers who were on in their years, musicians from the town band, seminarians and priests (it's easy to reawaken the faith of soldiers over whom death is hovering, leading them to pray, to confess, and thus prepare themselves for eternal happiness).

Rembrandt learned immediately that the main requirements of a good stretcher-bearer are delicacy and precision. Precision in the sense of the ability to walk at an even pace, in concert with one's partner, and to keep the stretcher as horizontal as possible. The steps to the entrance required special attention: you had to be careful to carry the stretcher headfirst when you were going up, and feetfirst when you were going down. Delicacy was needed when the stretcher was set down on the ground. And then there was a third quality that would come in handy for anyone equipped with it: resilience, if not a certain impermeability, before human suffering.

Atop the pink marble pavement of the Feestpaleis, where the wounded had been laid out, there was an uninterrupted coming and going of stretcher-bearers. When someone died, it was their job to wrap the corpse in a bedsheet and add it to the pile that was heaped in what until a short time before had been the animal cages.

Rembrandt had come to spend his whole day, every day, amid the moans and the howls of the suffering and the death rattle of the moribund, and he had learned that nothing is more consoling than the possibility of assisting one's fellow man in his moment of pain. But in his case it was a brief, temporary consolation.

THE ARTILLERY BARRAGE and the shots fired by two guns mounted on an armored train were not enough to hold the fortified positions. The flooding of the countryside around Antwerp slowed but did not halt the enemy's advance. The two defensive flanks were broken and finally collapsed, one after the other. On the night of October 7 the monstrous German howitzers took aim at the city. The Belgian cannons went silent before the enemy's superiority. On October 10 the mayor signed the capitulation of the city to the Germans.

Bugatti abandoned Antwerp. He traveled with a convoy that moved slowly over deeply-rutted dirt roads, coming across clusters of soldiers camped out by the sides of the ditches, crossing small towns that were almost unrecognizable in the darkness and the dust. After one day he arrived, in the morning, at the Ostend port, from where he embarked that same night for Dunkirk. And from Dunkirk he finally reached Paris.

There he spent a few weeks, just enough time to convince himself that even the elderly, women, children, and those exempt from the draft—the only ones, in other words, who had remained in the city—had the aura of people preparing to leave; enough time to realize that the houses, streets, and parks of Paris seemed familiar but were alien; enough time to notice that the Jardin des Plantes had been transformed into a desert. In the end Rembrandt took a decision: after ten years of being away, ten years in which, in truth, he had never lived with nostalgia or regret, he left Paris and returned to Italy.

Two days before his departure for Milan, Rembrandt paid a visit to Adrien Hébrard at his foundry on Avenue de Versailles.

The contract they had drawn up in earlier times was still valid: "Monsieur Bugatti agrees for a period of ___ years . . . not to cede any of his works to another foundry or art publisher . . . and to consign to Monsieur Hébrard, who will nevertheless be free . . . with exclusive rights . . ." etc., etc.

But the foundry had been closed for months. The ovens were extinguished, ovens whose mouths had issued masterpieces that earned Hébrard comparisons to the master founders of the Renaissance, works that some had compared to the bronzes buried beneath the ashes of Pompeii.

Even the doors to the gallery, whose windows looked onto Rue Royale, were barred. The rooms deserted and empty. The only thing left in the offices was a desk, behind which Bugatti found Hébrard, seated.

"Times are tough," Hébrard told him. "War destroys art. Did you hear of my father's death? Do you feel like having a bite to eat?" he asked.

Not far from Rue Royale there was a brasserie. It was a modest place, but with a couple of inside rooms where you could have a meal without running the risk of being disturbed. Bugatti and Hébrard headed in that direction.

"What will you have?" asked Hébrard.

"I think I'll have the leg of lamb," answered Rembrandt, after taking a quick glance at the menu.

"I thought you were a vegetarian. Didn't you used to say it was deplorable, shameful, to kill animals so we could gorge on their flesh and blood?"

"You're confusing me with Troubetzkoy," was Bugatti's curt reply.

"Anyway," Hébrard went on, "no one is interested in artworks anymore, whether paintings or sculpture, small or large. Not even in the colored terracotta statuettes that used to sell so well until last year. And even less in animal sculptures. Want to hear a story? The other week I needed a new pair of clippers to prune the plants in my garden, so I went to La Samaritaine department store. And who should I find amid the watering cans and rakes in the garden section? A man who looked like Pompon. François Pompon, the animal sculptor."

"I like Pompon," said Bugatti, "he's talented and brave. I've heard that he has himself locked inside the aviary with the birds he uses as models, not worrying that he might catch an infection from their feathers and droppings."

"That's him," continued Hébrard, "well there he was, Pompon, behind the counter, stacking up bags of fertilizer. At first I thought it couldn't be François, but rather his twin, Hector, whom I don't know, but whom I've heard mentioned. I didn't know that Hector had died six years ago. It's me, said Pompon, I don't have any more commissions. Before I used to make a living carving out blocks of marble for other sculptors. Now there's no more work. My wife is sick and it's hard to find anyone who wants to give a job to a man with white hair. And so, when this position opened up, I accepted immediately. The salary is good. Can you believe it?" concluded Hébrard, eating a piece of cake. "This is the situation."

In Milan Bugatti surrendered to the void, to ennui. There was no zoo in the city, only a few cages here and there in the Giardini Pubblici on Corso Venezia, with a giraffe, a leopard, a few deer, a monkey, and a few aging gazelles. The only friend he spent time with was Giulio Ulisse Arata, the architect and art critic. At first Rembrandt tried to see him every morning at his studio on Via Mascheroni. The studio, which also doubled as his home, was on the second floor of a building that Arata himself had designed (an elegant building, symmetrical, with a sober façade divided by pilasters with acanthus leaves and a moderate display of eclectic elements such as a double-vaulted balcony on the *piano nobile*. The building could not have been more unlike the gothic flights of fancy he would later design).

This is how Arata described those visits: "Rembrandt would enter the studio looking painfully sad and melancholic. He would come in without saying hello, without saying a word, and sink into an armchair and start complaining about how tired he felt. He would attempt to work. He would start a statue but not finish it, making and unmaking. Some days he would come to the studio only to destroy the work he had done the day before."

His appearances at Arata's studio became less and less frequent, tapering off until they ended completely. He confided to his friend that some nights he could only breathe by holding a damp handkerchief over his mouth. He could no longer stand Milan. He had the impression it was the city that kept him from shaking off the exhausting sadness and revulsion that had suffocated all his feelings.

At the beginning of the summer of 1915, Rembrandt returned to Paris. His father and mother had left the house on Rue Jeanne-d'Arc some time ago, and were now living in Pierrefonds-les-Bains. Carlo Bugatti had become mayor of that small town in Picardy, known for the therapeutic qualities of its sulphuric waters, which relieves ailments and aches and pains.

It was then that Rembrandt, looking for new lodgings that would also serve as a studio, ended up finding a two-room apartment, not very well-lit but large enough, at 3 Rue Joseph-Bara.

On the opposite side of the street, at number 6, his friend André Salmon lived in a small oblong room. Now he was at the Western Front, with the 26th battalion of the Light Infantry. Poet, writer, journalist, art critic, a few years earlier, in the pages of *Art et Décoration: Revue mensuelle d'Art Moderne*, he had compared Bugatti "to an ancient shepherd," who during his leisure time, rather than sculpt frolicking shepherdesses, preferred "to take as his subjects the sheep in his flock, his horses and his long-horned bulls." He called him an "animal sculptor by predestination." In closing he observed that even the few human figures Rembrandt had created were nothing more than "animals of a superior species."

VI

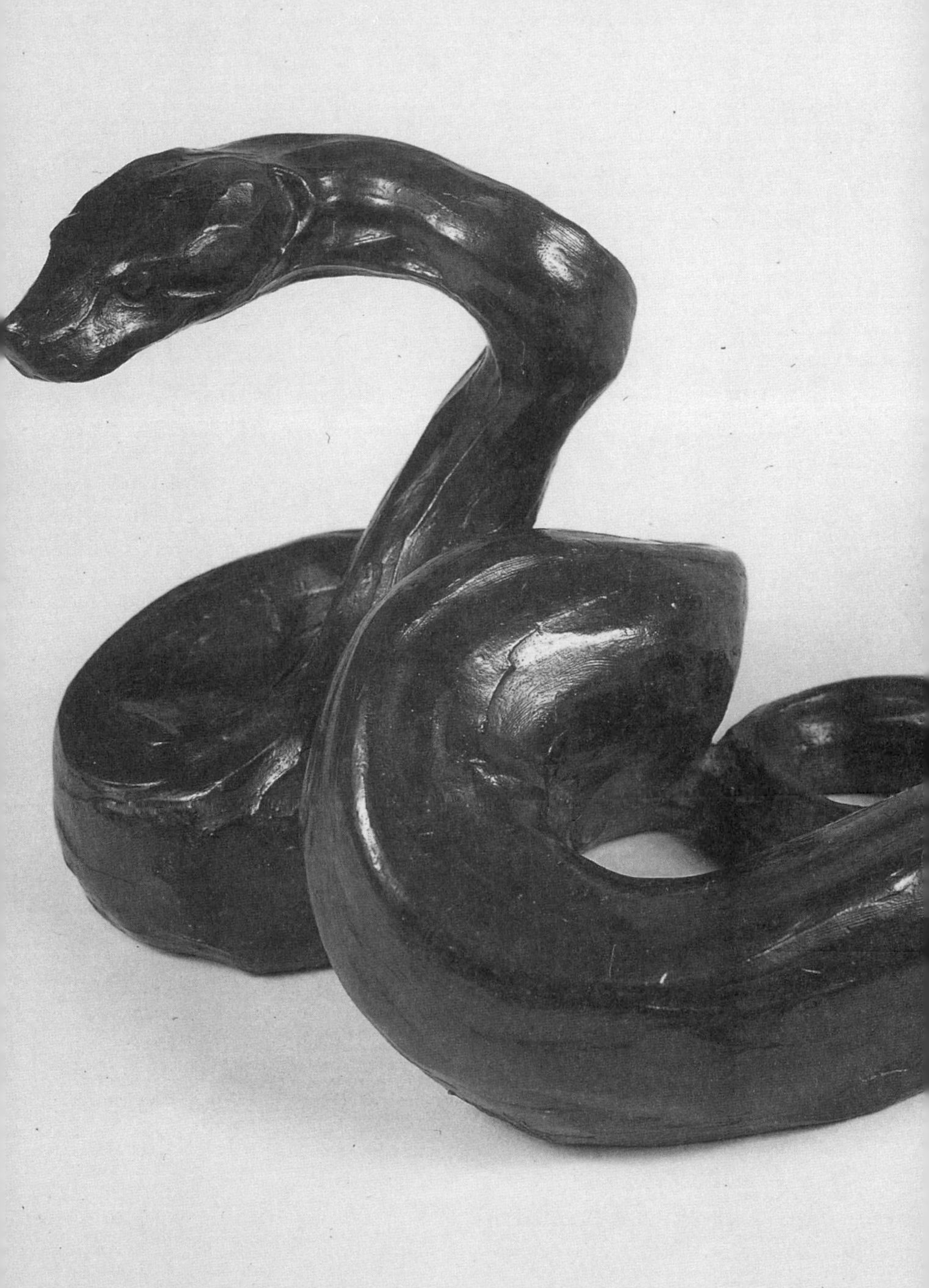

Ever since his return to Paris, Rembrandt had gone to Mass almost every morning, to the Église de la Madeleine, and at least once a week he had Père Galtier hear his confession.

He went to church that morning, too, and, at the end of the ceremony, Père Galtier saw Rembrandt make the sign of the cross and genuflect, and then head down the grand nave of the half-empty church, toward the vestibule. The priest was concerned. Strange rumors had reached his ears about his diligent penitent. He caught up with him and took him gently by one elbow, leading him toward the corner where the statue of Sainte Amélie is situated.

"My son," he said, "you and I must have a talk. The first thing I have to say to you is: man is progress, progress in every direction, do you understand? Can we say the same about the animals? Read the *Histoire Naturelle* by Buffon, read Ulisse Aldrovandi, read Pliny the Elder. Can you agree with me that sixteen centuries have not produced a single tangible change, a single significant step forward, in the manner of being or behaving that those great men observed for so long? Animals can see, hear sounds, smell, taste, touch things: yes. They can retain images, remember, dream, even discern what represents a danger to them: yes. But after that? Animals live and thus they have a soul, of course, and there is no difference between the nervous systems of animals and men, but as Saint Thomas or Saint Bonaventure argued—I don't remember which one right now—we must never forget that between the soul of man and the soul of animals there are three essential differences: first, their nature, second, their origin, and third . . . and third . . . why don't you tell me, my son."

Rembrandt pretended to search his memories for an answer to the question of Père Galtier, who after a few seconds of useless waiting resumed his speech.

"But fate!" he exclaimed. "Fate." And he added, lowering his voice, "*Intra fortunam debet quisque manere suam.* Every man should live within his own lot in life. We have to reject the idea that in animals there is any perception of the divine."

Then Père Galtier looked away from Rembrandt and, staring at the marble book that Sainte Amélie was holding, he said, "Although an animal may fear the unknown, that which seems supernatural to it—a rumbling in the woods, for example—this is no reason to assert that it possesses a religious sentiment. No, it cannot, because the religious sentiment presupposes the idea of religion, and the idea of religion," said Père Galtier, staring Rembrandt in the face and making a gesture as if to raise a finger in the air, "the idea of religion, my son, presupposes the idea of a being that is necessary, infinite, immutable, eternal, a sovereign and regnant being, the idea, in short, of God."

Rembrandt would like to have formulated a reply, perhaps winning the argument with a Latin quotation such as *talpae oculos possidetis* (you have the eyes of a mole), or *pulsate et aperietur vobis* (knock and the door will be opened), but he leaned his head slightly forward in assent. His face was tired as if he hadn't slept in weeks.

"Do you need to confess?" the priest asked him, smiling, with a slightly less pointed and expressive look.

"No, Father," Rembrandt replied.

"Alright, I have to leave you now. This morning I have a meeting with the young people of the Crusade," said Père Galtier. (To beg for God's intercession to bring an end to the war, the Archbishop of Paris had, in fact, come up with the idea of an army of children, of crusaders, as he called them, whom he organized in a rigidly hierarchical fashion. The corporals were obliged to receive communion once a month, the sergeants once a week, and the officers every day. In this army there were no mere foot soldiers.)

Rembrandt made the sign of the cross again, headed toward the exit and, pushing the door, left the church. It was eight o'clock in the morning, in the month of January. A milky haze covered the Rue Royale.

There was a man without a leg selling tricolor cockades, leaning against a column of La Madeleine and holding himself up with a crutch. Rembrandt recognized him: it was Monsieur Moussinac, the zookeeper from the Jardin des Plantes. A medal was pinned to the lapel of his coat. Rembrandt had grown thinner and more stooped. His face was pale, as white as ivory, in strange contrast with the vivid pink of his cheeks. It took the former zookeeper a few seconds to recognize the sculptor. But as soon as he did, he broke out in a smile and extended both hands toward him, holding himself up with one elbow on the crutch, and hobbling slightly.

"I went to the hospital at least five times," said Moussinac to Rembrandt, "and I showed what's left of my mangled leg to at least ten medical officials, but two months ago it finally arrived. Yes, I received a new leg! Nowadays they make amazing things, even masks with moveable jaws: you can't speak but at least you can chew. My new leg is a thing of beauty: a suction cup socket, oak, steel knee, a jointed foot. But I still have to get used to it. You have to take care of it, keep it clean. They recommend oiling it every day."

On the wall of one of the two rooms on Rue Joseph-Bara, the portrait taken by André Taponier was gone. In its place there was a large wooden cross that reached almost to the ceiling, although the base was propped against the floor. Rembrandt had nailed the two planks together himself. He recovered them one night on Boulevard de Clichy, where a fire had destroyed a building a few months earlier. The only thing that remained was rubble, charred and splintered beams and wall frames, iron rods, and wooden poles. This is not the time to do animals, he thought.

He found his Christ at a café in Montmartre. Antonio, if we must give him a name, had arrived in France two years earlier from a little village at the foot of Vesuvius, where he had been a construction worker. In his early days in Paris he worked at a soap factory. After they closed the factory he got by as best he could. He went to the wine market every day and for a few francs he would move around barrels that weighed a ton. From dawn to dusk he would fill bottles with Bourgogne and Crémant. He would wash the empties and divide them up: the Rhines to one side, the Burgundies to the other. He would scrub the casks, sweep the cellar.

Rembrandt explained to him what he had in mind, and Antonio answered, "For me it's just another job."

Not even when he found himself before the cross did he betray any misgivings, any hesitation, much less any second thoughts. He observed Rembrandt in silence while he ripped a sheet into three pieces and dipped one after the other in a bucket of water.

"Take off your clothes and shoes," he told him.

The young man stood there naked. Rembrandt took a second sheet, rolled it up loosely, and knotted it against his hip. Although it was only early autumn, the cold air was already creeping in, especially at night. Shivering, with his arms folded, the model went to a corner of the room while Rembrandt removed the cross from the wall, and positioned it at a slant. "Courage, my friend," Rembrandt told him, gesturing for him to come closer.

Antonio set his foot on the wedge that had been nailed a few inches above the bottom, leaned his shoulders against the crossbeam, and stretched out his arms. Rembrandt tied his wrists with the strips he had torn from the bedsheet. First one, then the other, forcefully.

"Now for your ankles," he said, kneeling down on the floor. Twice around and a nice knot. "Is it too tight?" he asked.

"That's how it's supposed to be, I think," replied Antonio.

Then, with a tremendous effort, Rembrandt pushed the cross up closer to the wall.

"There, just right!" he said, with sweat on his brow despite the cold. Then he turned the valve that regulated the flame of the gas lamp to cast a little more light. From the tabletop he took a lump of Plasticine, approached the armature already prepared in the middle of the room, and started to feverishly model his three-dimensional maquette, as he always did, but this time with the addition, perhaps, of even greater energy, even greater impatience. After about half an hour of this rough and tenacious struggle, this blunt assault, with his head lowered, his Christ started to become visibly distressed, to twist his torso, to push his shoulders upward to relieve the tension on the muscles of his chest and abdomen, and to emit muffled groans.

When Rembrandt untied him from the cross and

helped him to lie down on the floor, his hands and feet were swollen and he was struggling to breathe. The cloth strips had left deep, purple marks on his wrists and ankles.

With one of the strips Rembrandt delicately dried the cold sweat that coated his face and chest and the rest of his body.

"It's only cramps," said the man with a vulnerable smile.

"Cramps," repeated Rembrandt, unpersuaded.

A few minutes later Antonio was once again on the cross, his arms outstretched and his knees slightly bent, his hands and feet bound to the two boards. Once again Rembrandt pushed the cross and the body hanging from it against the wall, struggling to get it perfectly upright.

The whole process was repeated five more times over the course of the night: when the model was on the verge of collapse, Rembrandt would lower the large cross from the wall, untie the man, place his hands beneath his armpits, lay him down on the floor, and without saying a word stand there observing him, waiting for him to recover. Antonio would stare at the ceiling for a few minutes, breathing deeply. Then he would sit up, rub his wrists and ankles with his hands and, making a gesture with his head that seemed to be contradicted by the expression in his eyes, he would tell Rembrandt that he was ready again.

It was almost dawn when at the end of one of these pauses, Antonio, still full of zeal and goodwill, or maybe simply patient acquiescence, indicated that he could resume the pose. Rembrandt finally announced to him instead that the maquette was finished. He then added that he didn't have a franc to pay him, and would give him in exchange one of his precious shirts or a pair of trousers, maybe a jacket. "Or would you prefer a pair of shoes?" he asked, pointing to the ones on his feet. The other man furrowed his brow, ready to protest. But a second later he shrugged his shoulders.

"My fault. I should have known," he grumbled. "When I arrived, I immediately thought that if such an elegant gentleman lives in a rat's nest like this, it means he hasn't got a cent. So be it. I'll take the shoes."

Rembrandt removed his shoes and handed them over.

"A little big," said Antonio, after trying them on, slipping a finger behind his tendon. Only then did Rembrandt notice how small and boney the man's hands were.

"We'll leave it at that," said Antonio, "now I really need a bed."

VII

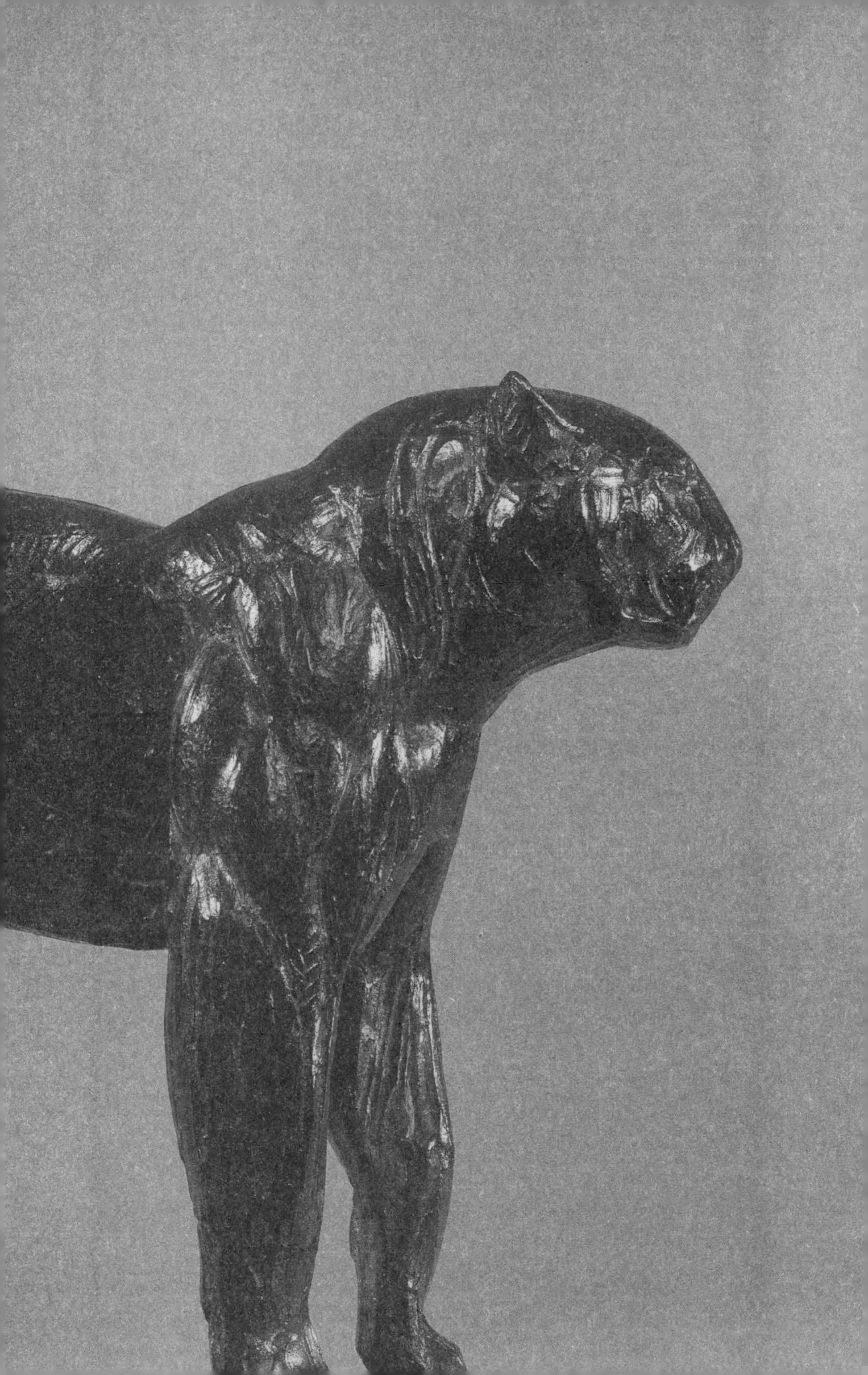

Saturday, January 8, 1916. Early morning. The bitter cold of winter had left the streets icy and Rembrandt Bugatti's gait was even more stiff and uncertain than usual. At the corner of Faubourg Saint-Honoré, a woman made a timid gesture of offering him a small bouquet of violets.

"For you, monsieur. You like flowers, don't you?"

Rembrandt accepted the bouquet of violets and gave the woman a coin. "I always take this street but I've never run into you before," he said.

"It's the first time I've come here," replied the flower woman, "usually I'm in the area of Notre-Dame. You're not French, are you, monsieur?"

"No," replied Bugatti.

After crossing the Pont de la Concorde and leaving behind the Seine, on which gray chunks of ice were floating, Rembrandt turned into Boulevard Raspail. From the sky there was a diaphanous light, and touching his felt hat with his fingertips Rembrandt felt moisture on the brim. Passing by a newsstand he stopped for a moment to look at the photographs of horses in the war zone on the front page of a daily newspaper. Their heads were covered with gas masks. Shuddering in his overcoat, he moved on.

By the entry to 3 Rue Joseph-Bara, Madame Soulimant was seated as usual.

"Good morning," she said with a sleepy smile.

"Good morning, Madame Soulimant," replied Rembrandt.

"Where have you been," asked the custodian, who couldn't help but notice that on her tenant's cheek, which was generally so smooth and perfectly shaven, there was the shadow of a beard.

"At La Madeleine," replied Rembrandt, in a voice without affect.

"At this hour of the morning?"

"Yes, at the first Mass."

"What lovely violets, Monsieur Bugatti."

"I bought them from a woman who sells them on Faubourg Saint-Honoré," said Rembrandt, placing them near his nose.

"The flower that can resist the winter cold," said Madame Soulimant. "They'll make the whole house smell nice."

I'll need water for these violets, thought Rembrandt while he climbed the stairs up to his lodgings.

Behind the doors of the other apartments you could hear whispering and muffled sounds. People had just woken up. On the whitewashed walls of the landing, where the paint was peeling, the damp had caused green stains to form that resembled big cabbages. Water and a glass, he thought to himself. And in fact, the first thing he did, once he had closed the door to his apartment and even before taking off his coat, was to look for a glass on the table, which was still littered with leftovers from the night before, in addition to spatulas, files, a palette knife, sticks, and the shreds of Plasticine. After rinsing out the dried dregs from a wineglass, Rembrandt placed the bouquet in the glass and set it in front of a dirty window, beyond which all you could see was the blank wall of the building opposite. Then he removed his overcoat and hat and placed them inside the closet, where jackets, vests, and trousers had been carelessly hung.

I have to straighten up this place, he said to himself, I have to get rid of the clutter on this table.

Clearing the table quickly and making a little space, he took some stationery, a pen, and ink from the dresser drawer. Then he sat down at the table and started to write. He wrote three letters.

The first was to a couple he knew who lived outside of Paris. Some time back they had asked whether they might visit the place where he worked. Struggling to maintain a serious composure he proposed that they of course come to see him the next week, when they would be more than welcome.

The second letter was addressed to his brother: "Ettore Bugatti—Grand-Hôtel—Boulevard des Capucines, Paris." Who knows whether Rembrandt advised him, once again, to be "a bastard with men, a gentleman to women, and God to children," but always "good to animals." More than a few conjectures have been made about this letter, and more than one fantasy, but its contents are still completely unknown today.

The last was for the police commissioner of the neighborhood: "January 8, 1916. To the Police Commissioner of the Notre-Dame-des-Champs quarter. Dear Sir, My gesture . . ."

LEANING AGAINST THE back of a chair, he noticed the rags he had used to tie to the cross the Italian whom he had met in the fall in Montmartre. Rembrandt took them and tore them into thin strips, meticulously, one by one. Then, with a fastidious slowness, he tucked them around the window frames and in the cracks between the door and the floor, sealing off every opening.

Inside a pan he boiled a little water over the gas. He decided to shave. In front of a mirror barely big enough to show his face, he checked the part in his hair. The razor glided over his cheeks, his chin, and, delicately, around his mouth. When it reached his neck, at the height of his prominent Adam's apple, Rembrandt may have hesitated, had a moment of uncertainty. But otherwise why would I have done all this work, so precisely, so diligently, with the strips of cloth? he thought, gazing at the islands of foam that floated on the water in the washbasin. When he finished shaving, he calmly dried his face and went to the closet.

What should he wear? Without giving it too much thought, perhaps because he had imagined this moment many times, he took out a dark suit, an ivory vest, the last shirt he had picked up from the laundry, and a burgundy tie, and he laid them on the bed. In the back of the closet a pair of single-button, white cotton gloves almost completely concealed a small dark blue case. Rembrandt took the gloves and the case—on which the initials R.F. were embossed in gold letters—and set them next to his outfit.

Outside the dirty windows the winter fog turned the air gray, leaving the room dark though it was already midmorning. Footsteps and voices echoed from the stairwell.

Rembrandt walked over to the brass lamp that was hanging from the ceiling and opened the valve to the maximum. He stopped for a second to listen to the hissing of the gas.

WHEN THE POLICE commissioner of the quarter, a certain Lompré, entered Rembrandt's apartment, followed by a weeping Madame Soulimant, it was late afternoon.

"The window," he instructed the agent accompanying him. Then, covering his nose and mouth with one hand, he closed the valve of the lamp.

Rembrandt was lying on the bed, impeccably dressed. On his hands, which were crossed over his stomach, he was wearing the white gloves. On his feet, which protruded past the edge of the bed, he had on a pair of patent leather shoes with square toes.

The smell of gas was overwhelming and caught in the throat. Lompré bent over and placed his ear on Rembrandt's chest. "Did you call a doctor?" he asked the concierge.

"Doctor Villesboniet, who lives next door," replied Madame Soulimant.

On the small nightstand by the bed were the envelopes with the three letters, a glass holding the violets with their now withered petals, and a dark blue case against which were gleaming the gold initials of the République Française.

Lompré opened the case. Lifting up a small red ribbon with two fingers, he observed for a second the insignia of the *Légion d'honneur*, the five-armed Maltese Cross, in silver plate enameled white. Then he gingerly replaced it in the case.

"One is for you, commissioner," said the agent, handing him the envelopes.

The commissioner opened the letter that Rembrandt had addressed to him. A few lines that Lompré read without betraying any emotion. In the meantime the doctor had arrived. He approached the bed, looked at the outstretched man, and said, "He's too long for the coffin."

"His heart is still beating," said the commissioner.

"Yes, it's still beating," confirmed Doctor Villesboinet, removing an immaculate handkerchief from the breast pocket of his jacket and forcefully opening Rembrandt's mouth.

"There's a car downstairs. We're taking him to Laennec's."

Then, with his fingers wrapped in the handkerchief he grabbed hold of Rembrandt's tongue and started to pull it. Short repeated tugs.

"There's no time for mouth-to-mouth resuscitation," said Villesboinet to the commissioner, who was only half listening, drawn as he was to the enormous wooden cross against the wall, in the advancing darkness of the room.

BUGATTI'S BODY, STILL hanging on to life, arrived a short time later at the hospital that bore the name of René-Théophile-Hyacinthe Laennec, the inventor of the stethoscope.

At first air was pumped into his lungs with an artificial ventilation machine, then he was bled, and finally he was given a shot of camphor oil (Villesboinet's suggestion of cold compresses on the neck was ignored). Rembrandt Bugatti, without ever regaining consciousness, passed away during the course of the night.

Two days later, *Le Petit Parisien* published a long article, *Mort dramatique du sculpteur R. Bugatti*, in which the reasons for his suicide were generically indicated as the atrocities and horrors of the war. To read the most emotional and perhaps most exact obituary of Rembrandt one would have to wait for the words of Giulio Ulisse Arata who, a few weeks later, wrote in the pages of an art magazine published in Milan, "Bugatti lived life as a stranger, and he died as an unknown man erasing behind him every trace of his existence."

The Funeral Mass was celebrated at ten o'clock in the morning on Thursday, January 13, in Notre-Dame-des-Champs. Although when confronted by those who deliberately take their own lives—out of revulsion at life, to escape from scandal or illness, or maybe out of a morbid fury at the void—the Church did not, as a rule, provide for a Christian funeral and burial; in the case of Bugatti, "in consideration of the fairly subtle canon law," as acknowledged by Cardinal Amette, the Archbishop of Paris, an exception was granted. This unusual, and in certain respects unexpected decision of Monsignor Amette left an impression on the few persons who gathered for the ceremony in Notre-Dame-des-Champs. During his homily, the celebrant, Abbé Genevray, did not fail to remark that funeral services should be considered above all a sign of compassion, an appeal for divine intercession for the salvation of the soul, and ultimately, nevertheless, a mystery of the faith. The following day the corpse of Rembrandt Bugatti was transported to Milan. Beneath a violent downpour, in the presence of his father, his mother, his brother, Ettore, his sister-in-law and his nieces and nephews, his body was buried without ceremony in the family plot. Only after the war would it be exhumed to be buried in Dorlisheim, where it rests today alongside the other four men who bear his same name.

AUTHOR'S NOTE

To WRITE THIS story I consulted many books, including the following, which I found particularly helpful: Boniface de Castellane, *L'Art d'être pauvre. Mémoires*, G. Crès et Cie, Paris, 1925; Jacques-Chalom Des Cordes and Véronique Fromanger Des Cordes, *Rembrandt Bugatti. Catalogue raisonné*, Les Éditions de l'Amateur, Paris, 1987; Philippe Dejean, *Carlo, Rembrandt, Ettore, Jean Bugatti*, Rizzoli International Publications, New York, 1982; André Demaison, *Le Livre des enfants sauvages*, André Bonne, Paris, 1953; Remy de Gourmont, *Epilogues. Réflexions sur la vie. Volume complémentaire: 1905-1912*, Mercure de France, Paris, 1913; Edward Horswell, *Rembrandt Bugatti: Life in Sculpture*, Sladmore Gallery Editions, London, 2004; Paul Léautaud, *Journal littéraire*, Mercure de France, Paris, vol. I: 1893-1906, 1954; and André Salmon, *Souvenirs sans fin*, Gallimard, Paris, vol. II: *Deuxième époque (1908-1920)*, 1956.

LIST OF ILLUSTRATIONS

Edgardo Franzosini, born in 1952 near Lake Como, is the author of five novels. *The Animal Gazer* won two distinguished Italian literary awards in 2016, the Premio Comisso and the Premio Dessi. He lives in Milan.

Michael F. Moore has translated works by Alessandro Manzoni, Alberto Moravia and Primo Levi. Prior to becoming an interpreter at the Permanent Mission of Italy to the United Nations, he studied sculpture at the Brera Academy in Milan.

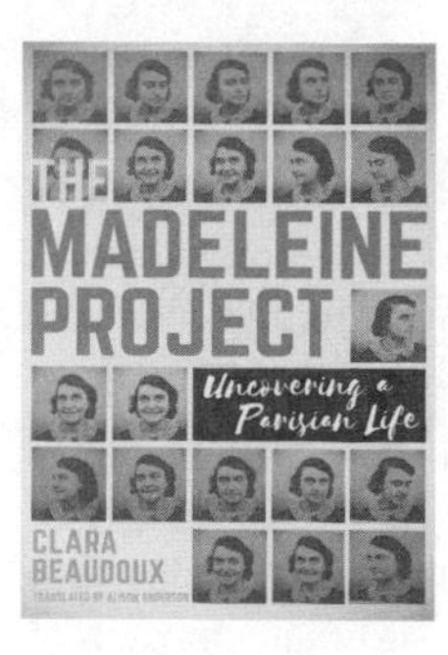

***The Madeleine Project* by Clara Beaudoux**

A young woman moves into a Paris apartment and discovers a storage room filled with the belongings of the previous owner, a certain Madeleine who died in her late nineties, and whose treasured possessions nobody seems to want. In an audacious act of journalism driven by personal curiosity and humane tenderness, Clara Beaudoux embarks on *The Madeleine Project*, documenting what she finds on Twitter with text and photographs, introducing the world to an unsung 20th century figure.

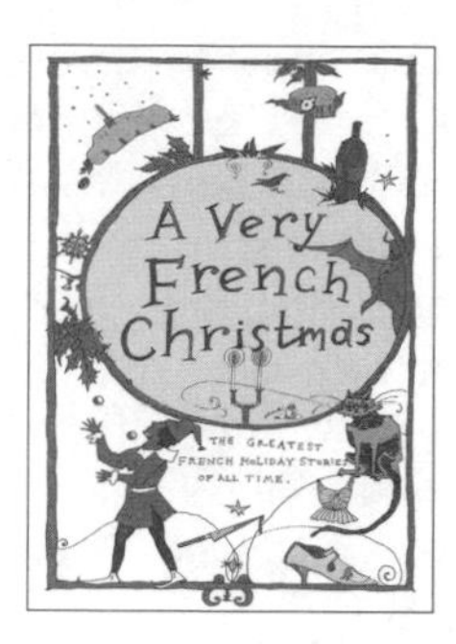

A Very French Christmas

A continuation of the very popular Very Christmas Series, this collection brings together the best French Christmas stories of all time in an elegant and vibrant collection featuring classics by Guy de Maupassant and Alphonse Daudet, plus stories by the esteemed twentieth century author Irène Némirovsky and contemporary writers Dominique Fabre and Jean-Philippe Blondel. With a holiday spirit conveyed through sparkling Paris streets, opulent feasts, wandering orphans, flickering desire, and more than a little wine, this collection proves that the French have mastered Christmas.

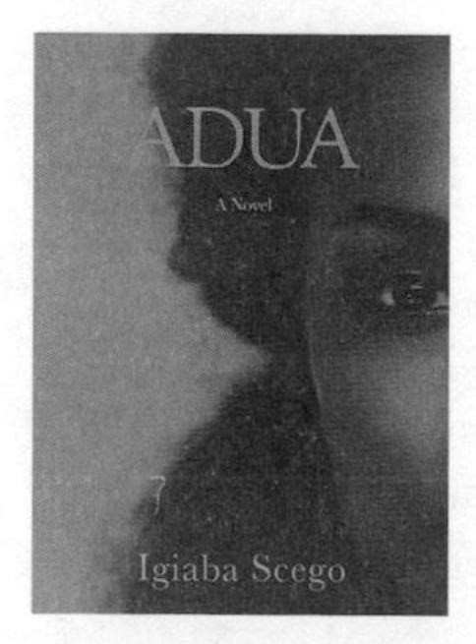

***Adua* by Igiaba Scego**

Adua, an immigrant from Somalia to Italy, has lived in Rome for nearly forty years. She came seeking freedom from a strict father and an oppressive regime, but her dreams of film stardom ended in shame. Now that the civil war in Somalia is over, her homeland calls her. She must decide whether to return and reclaim her inheritance, but also how to take charge of her own story and build a future.

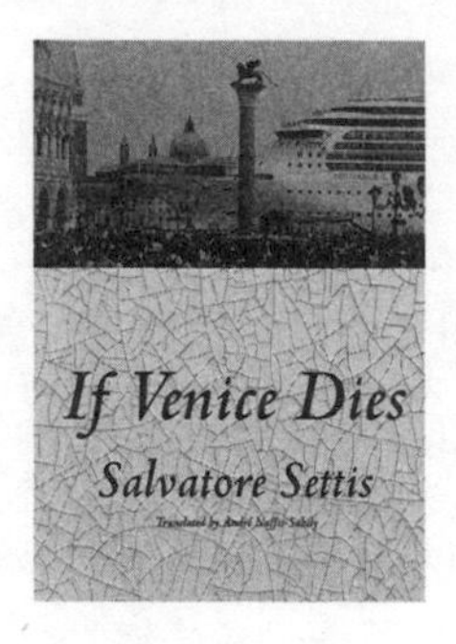

***If Venice Dies* by Salvatore Settis**
Internationally renowned art historian Salvatore Settis ignites a new debate about the Pearl of the Adriatic and cultural patrimony at large. In this fiery blend of history and cultural analysis, Settis argues that "hit-and-run" visitors are turning Venice and other landmark urban settings into shopping malls and theme parks. This is a passionate plea to secure the soul of Venice, written with consummate authority, wide-ranging erudition and élan.

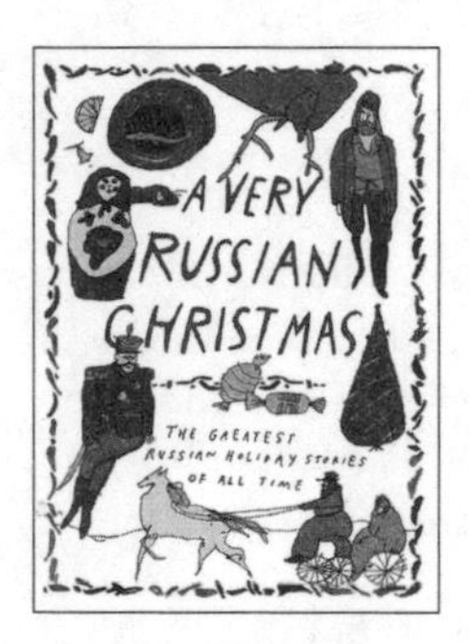

A Very Russian Christmas
This is Russian Christmas celebrated in supreme pleasure and pain by the greatest of writers, from Dostoevsky and Tolstoy to Chekhov and Teffi. The dozen stories in this collection will satisfy every reader, and with their wit, humor, and tenderness, packed full of sentimental songs, footmen, whirling winds, solitary nights, snow drifts, and hopeful children, the collection proves that Nobody Does Christmas Like the Russians.

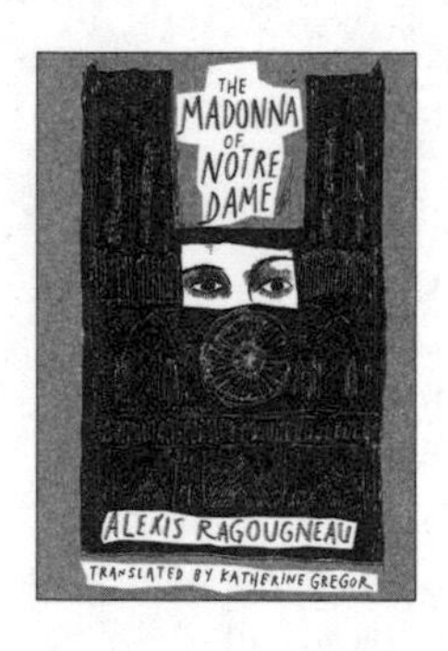

The Madonna of Notre Dame
by Alexis Ragougneau
Fifty thousand people jam into Notre Dame Cathedral to celebrate the Feast of the Assumption. The next morning, a beautiful young woman clothed in white kneels at prayer in a cathedral side chapel. But when someone accidentally bumps against her, her body collapses. She has been murdered. This thrilling novel illuminates shadowy corners of the world's most famous cathedral, shedding light on good and evil with suspense, compassion and wry humor.

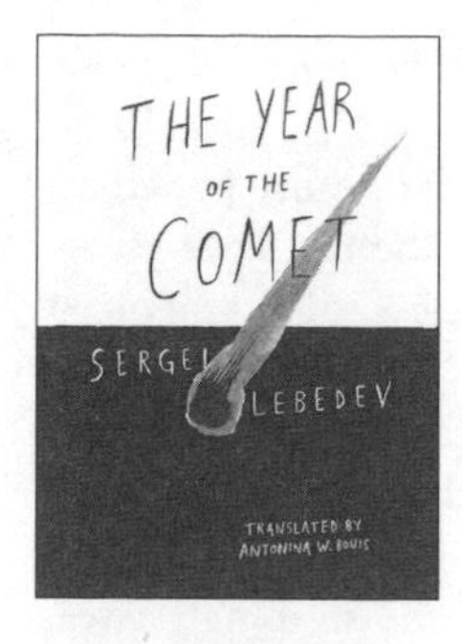

The Year of the Comet
by Sergei Lebedev

A story of a Russian boyhood and coming of age as the Soviet Union is on the brink of collapse. Lebedev depicts a vast empire coming apart at the seams, transforming a very public moment into something tender and personal, and writes with stunning beauty and shattering insight about childhood and the growing consciousness of a boy in the world.

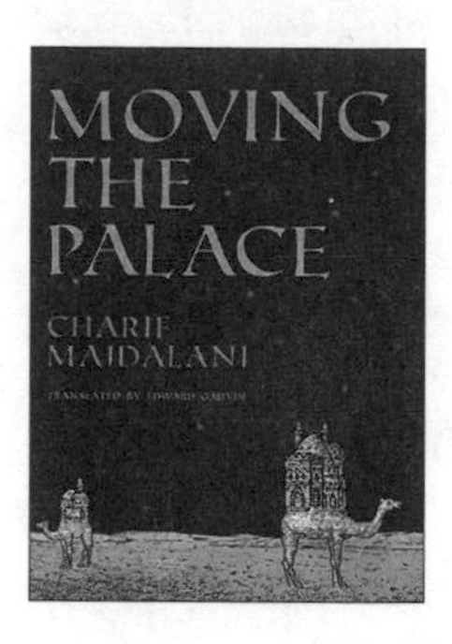

Moving the Palace
by Charif Majdalani

A young Lebanese adventurer explores the wilds of Africa, encountering an eccentric English colonel in Sudan and enlisting in his service. In this lush chronicle of far-flung adventure, the military recruit crosses paths with a compatriot who has dismantled a sumptuous palace and is transporting it across the continent on a camel caravan. This is a captivating modern-day Odyssey in the tradition of Bruce Chatwin and Paul Theroux.

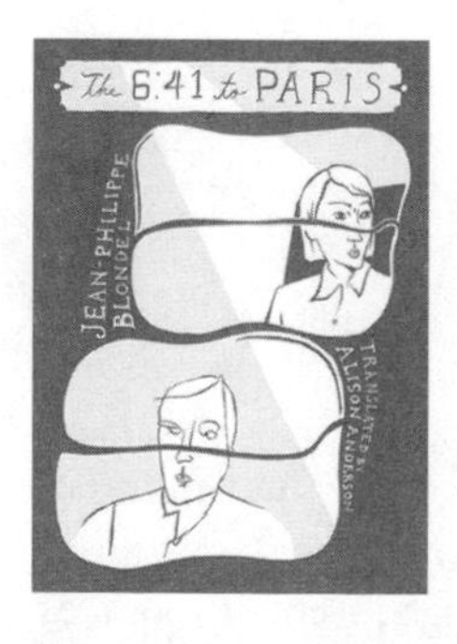

The 6:41 to Paris
by Jean-Philippe Blondel

Cécile, a stylish 47-year-old, has spent the weekend visiting her parents outside Paris. By Monday morning, she's exhausted. These trips back home are stressful and she settles into a train compartment with an empty seat beside her. But it's soon occupied by a man she recognizes as Philippe Leduc, with whom she had a passionate affair that ended in her brutal humiliation 30 years ago. In the fraught hour and a half that ensues, Cécile and Philippe hurtle towards the French capital in a psychological thriller about the pain and promise of past romance.

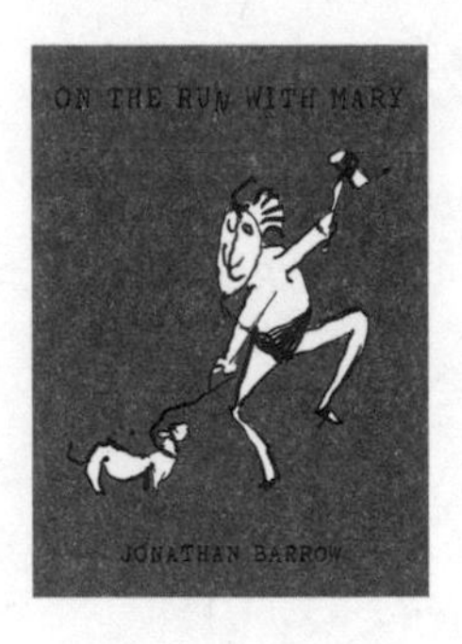

On the Run with Mary by Jonathan Barrow

Shining moments of tender beauty punctuate this story of a youth on the run after escaping from an elite English boarding school. At London's Euston Station, the narrator meets a talking dachshund named Mary and together they're off on escapades through posh Mayfair streets and jaunts in a Rolls-Royce. But the youth soon realizes that the seemingly sweet dog is a handful; an alcoholic, nymphomaniac, drug-addicted mess who can't stay out of pubs or off the dance floor. *On the Run with Mary* mirrors the horrors and the joys of the terrible 20th century.

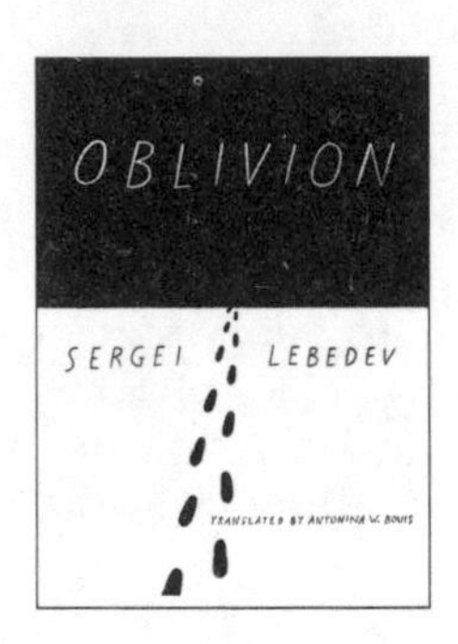

Oblivion by Sergei Lebedev

In one of the first 21st century Russian novels to probe the legacy of the Soviet prison camp system, a young man travels to the vast wastelands of the Far North to uncover the truth about a shadowy neighbor who saved his life, and whom he knows only as Grandfather II. Emerging from today's Russia, where the ills of the past are being forcefully erased from public memory, this masterful novel represents an epic literary attempt to rescue history from the brink of oblivion.

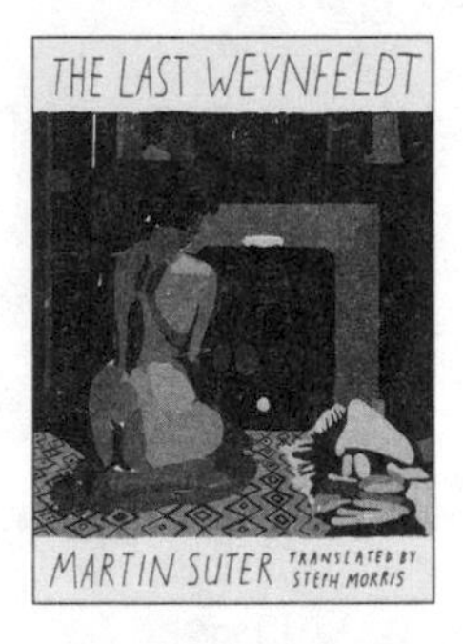

The Last Weynfeldt by Martin Suter

Adrian Weynfeldt is an art expert in an international auction house, a bachelor in his mid-fifties living in a grand Zurich apartment filled with costly paintings and antiques. Always correct and well-mannered, he's given up on love until one night—entirely out of character for him—Weynfeldt decides to take home a ravishing but unaccountable young woman and gets embroiled in an art forgery scheme that threatens his buttoned up existence. This refined page-turner moves behind elegant bourgeois facades into darker recesses of the heart.

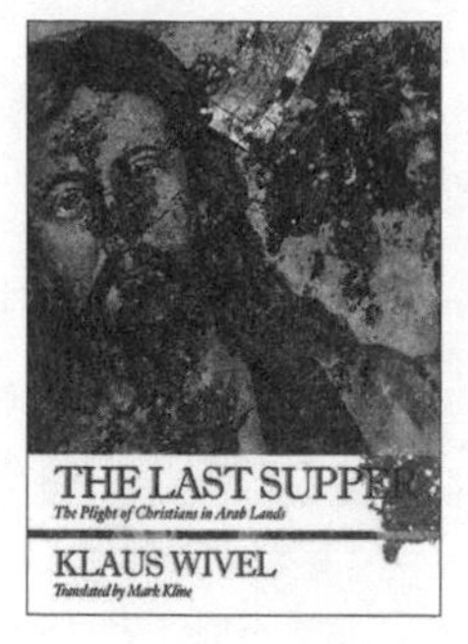

***The Last Supper* by Klaus Wivel**

Alarmed by the oppression of 7.5 million Christians in the Middle East, journalist Klaus Wivel traveled to Iraq, Lebanon, Egypt, and the Palestinian territories to learn about their fate. He found a minority under threat of death and humiliation, desperate in the face of rising Islamic extremism and without hope their situation will improve. An unsettling account of a severely beleaguered religious group living, so it seems, on borrowed time. Wivel asks, Why have we not done more to protect these people?

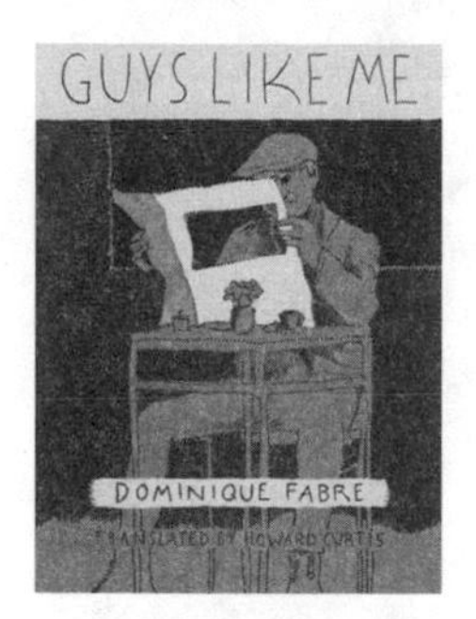

***Guys Like Me* by Dominique Fabre**

Dominique Fabre, born in Paris and a lifelong resident of the city, exposes the shadowy, anonymous lives of many who inhabit the French capital. In this quiet, subdued tale, a middle-aged office worker, divorced and alienated from his only son, meets up with two childhood friends who are similarly adrift. He's looking for a second act to his mournful life, seeking the harbor of love and a true connection with his son. Set in palpably real Paris streets that feel miles away from the City of Light, a stirring novel of regret and absence, yet not without a glimmer of hope.

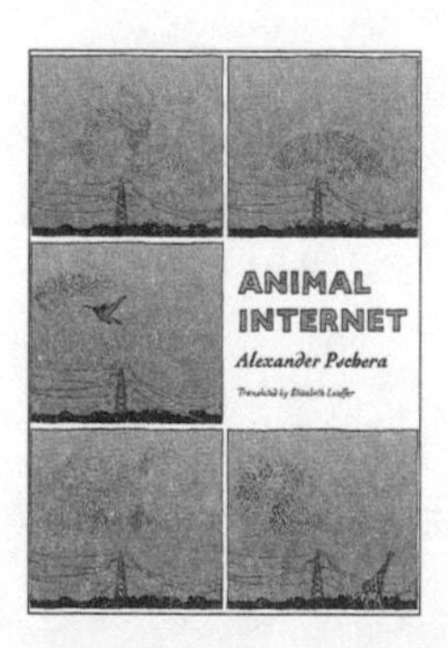

***Animal Internet* by Alexander Pschera**

Some 50,000 creatures around the globe—including whales, leopards, flamingoes, bats and snails—are being equipped with digital tracking devices. The data gathered and studied by major scientific institutes about their behavior will warn us about tsunamis, earthquakes and volcanic eruptions, but also radically transform our relationship to the natural world. Contrary to pessimistic fears, author Alexander Pschera sees the Internet as creating a historic opportunity for a new dialogue between man and nature.

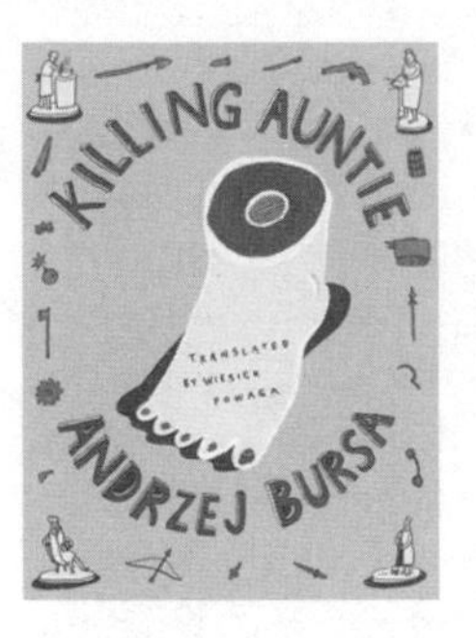

Killing Auntie by Andrzej Bursa

A young university student named Jurek, with no particular ambitions or talents, finds himself with nothing to do. After his doting aunt asks the young man to perform a small chore, he decides to kill her for no good reason other than, perhaps, boredom. This short comedic masterpiece combines elements of Dostoevsky, Sartre, Kafka, and Heller, coming together to produce an unforgettable tale of murder and—just maybe—redemption.

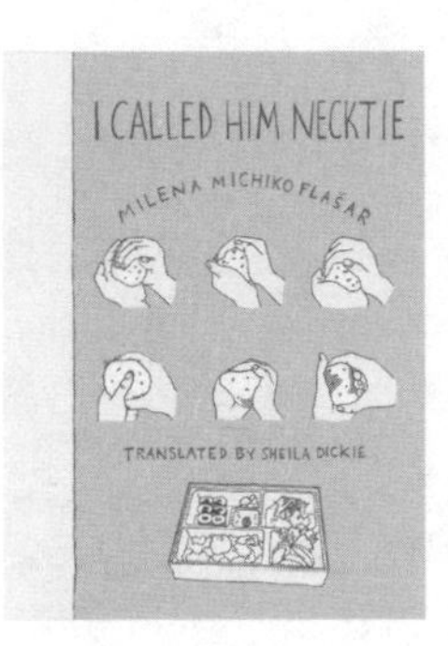

I Called Him Necktie by Milena Michiko Flašar

Twenty-year-old Taguchi Hiro has spent the last two years of his life living as a hikikomori—a shut-in who never leaves his room and has no human interaction—in his parents' home in Tokyo. As Hiro tentatively decides to reenter the world, he spends his days observing life from a park bench. Gradually he makes friends with Ohara Tetsu, a salaryman who has lost his job. The two discover in their sadness a common bond. This beautiful novel is moving, unforgettable, and full of surprises.

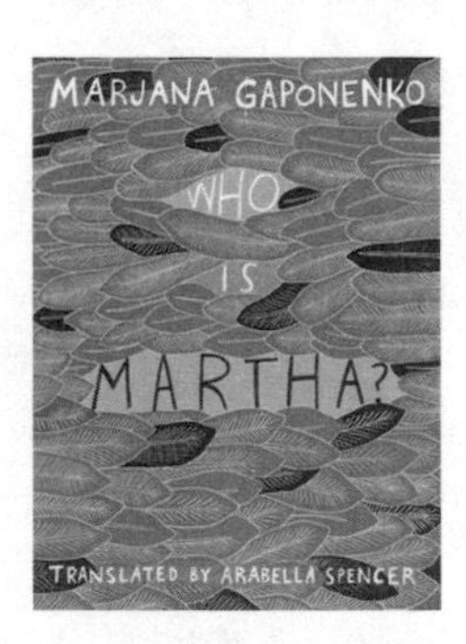

Who is Martha? by Marjana Gaponenko

In this rollicking novel, 96-year-old ornithologist Luka Levadski foregoes treatment for lung cancer and moves from Ukraine to Vienna to make a grand exit in a luxury suite at the Hotel Imperial. He reflects on his past while indulging in Viennese cakes and savoring music in a gilded concert hall. Levadski was born in 1914, the same year that Martha—the last of the now-extinct passenger pigeons—died. Levadski himself has an acute sense of being the last of a species. This gloriously written tale mixes piquant wit with lofty musings about life, friendship, aging and death.